SECRETS
IN A SMALL TOWN

SECRETS
IN A SMALL TOWN

by

Nicole Stiling

2019

SECRETS IN A SMALL TOWN

ISBN 13: 978-1-63555-436-6

This Trade Paperback Original Is Published By
Bold Strokes Books, Inc.
P.O. Box 249
Valley Falls, NY 12185

First Edition: May 2019

CREDITS
Editors: Victoria Villaseñor and Barbara Ann Wright
Production Design: Stacia Seaman
Cover Design by Jeanine Henning

Acknowledgments

First, I'd like to thank the team at Bold Strokes Books for taking a chance on an unknown and turning my dream into a page-turning reality.

To my editor, Victoria, thank you for editing me to within an inch of my life. This book is infinitely better because of you.

So much love and gratitude to my wife, Donna, for her steadfast support and ideas throughout the process. This would have been impossible without you.

To my children, I hope you see that it's possible to get anywhere you set your mind to, no matter how long the road is to get there.

Thank you to my family—Mom, Dad, Dad, Di, Nana, Grandpa, and everyone else who encouraged me along the way. I am forever grateful for your support.

For my mother—my harshest critic, my strongest supporter, and my closest friend. I love you with all my heart.

CHAPTER ONE

Their eyes darted back and forth as the Sig Sauer P226 waved slowly in front of them. The shine on the oiled black metal had them captivated; no one dared to look away. Sweat beaded on her forehead. She'd never been in control of so many at one time. If any of them, just *one* of them, decided to go rogue, she'd be at their mercy.

A hand shot up into the air. "Do you get free sodas at the 24/7 downtown?"

Relief began to creep in. Maybe Micki could handle this after all. "No, but some places offer discounts to police officers. I think the 24/7 takes a dollar off the total price."

Another hand wriggled in the air. "Do you really eat doughnuts all the time?"

"Um, no. We don't. Sometimes we bring doughnuts in to share, but we don't do it every day or anything."

The first-grade class at Winter Valley Elementary hung on Micki's every word, rapt. This was her first career day since becoming the deputy chief of police, and it was right up there with drug busts and fistfights.

A tiny boy with a buzz cut raised his hand. "My dad tells me that the police are going to put me in jail if I unbuckle my seat belt while he's driving. Is that true?"

Micki squirmed, not interested in creating family drama

by telling kids their parents were lying to them. "Well, no, not exactly, but you definitely should never do that. If your dad got into an accident, you could get seriously hurt."

The dam broke, and questions were shot at her from every direction.

"Can I touch your gun?"

"No."

"Can I hold your handcuffs?"

"No."

"Can we tie you up with a jump rope so you can show us how to break out of it?"

"Definitely not."

"Have you shot anybody?"

"Not today."

One of the students who Micki actually knew raised her hand politely. "Yes, Eliana?"

"Ryan doesn't believe that you're my friend. He thinks I'm making it up."

Micki smiled. "Actually, Ryan, Eliana's right. We *are* friends. She's my junior deputy," she said, throwing a wink to the small brunette. She grinned back, showing off the bare bit of gums where her two bottom teeth had recently fallen out.

"Well, if no one else has any questions, I think my time is just about up," Micki said. She pulled a bag of plastic police badges out from under her chair. "Any takers?"

The entire class jumped up from their seats and swarmed her. Micki turned sheepishly to the first-grade teacher, who was looking at her sternly.

"I thought we agreed that I would pass those out after your presentation."

"Sorry, Mrs. Gross. My bad."

The students were affixing their badges to their shirts, their belt loops, and their backpacks. Micki felt a sense of pride that they all thought her work was important. They didn't need to know that in such a small town, the most exciting thing that had happened in the last week was a stolen wallet. And it was later found in the owner's trunk.

"Let's give a round of applause to Chief Blake," Mrs. Gross said, starting it herself. The kids dutifully clapped while Micki waved good-bye.

Rebecca Raye was standing in the doorway, clapping along with the children. "Very nice, Chief."

"Did you see the whole thing?" Micki asked, tightening her belt once they were out in the hallway. Police belts were meant to stay put, but they couldn't stand up to a bunch of children pulling at handcuff cases and flashlights.

"No, just the end. Mrs. Gross was pissed at you."

"I seem to have that effect on teachers."

"You want some chicken nuggets? I have extras. It's the students' favorite lunch day. Besides pizza, of course."

Micki paused. "Yeah, I could eat."

She followed Rebecca down the long corridor to the cafeteria kitchen. Micki tied her hair into a ponytail to avoid getting any in the food. She plucked a wavy blond strand off her sleeve and held it over into the trash can, making sure it wasn't one of the gray ones she'd seen popping up lately. She was glad Rebecca hadn't asked her to put on a hairnet.

"Chicken nuggets again?" a voice asked from behind them.

"Oh, hi, Savannah," Rebecca said. "Yeah, that's our usual Thursday lunch. The kids love it."

Savannah Castillo held up a nugget, though she didn't look as if she actually wanted to touch it. "They also love cotton candy and ice cream, but neither of those things are appropriate lunches."

Rebecca cleared her throat. "We use all-natural chicken breast, and we bake them, so they're not really unhealthy."

Micki popped one into her mouth. "Mmm, delicious. And I can taste the healthiness with every bite," she said, looking pointedly at Savannah.

"Aren't you due back at the police station? I didn't realize an elementary school career presentation lasted an entire day." Savannah pulled the sunglasses from the top of her head and dangled them from her fingertips.

"Aren't you supposed to be at the town hall? I didn't realize that the town manager's agenda included an inspection of every public building in Winter Valley." Every single time she and Savannah faced off, Micki felt the need to get the last word in, which wasn't her style. But something about Savannah brought out her biting sarcasm.

"Actually, I—"

Rebecca interrupted. "Lunch is going to be served in fifteen minutes. If I don't get these plated up, we're going to have a mutiny on our hands. Savannah, I'll see you at five?"

It was clear Micki had been dismissed as Savannah turned her attention to Rebecca. Savannah nodded. "Yes. Please make sure all of her homework is done. Yesterday, she still had math to do when she got home."

"Absolutely. Sorry about that. I'll make sure Eliana finishes everything before you pick her up."

Savannah nodded and walked out of the cafeteria without another word.

"I think she likes me," Micki said, stuffing another chicken nugget into her mouth.

Rebecca laughed. "Do you have to antagonize her *all* the time? I think your life would be a whole lot easier if you just let things go once in a while."

"Nah. Where's the fun in that? You working at the diner tonight?" Micki asked, shrugging on her windbreaker.

"No, not tonight. Once Savannah picks up El, I'm just going to chill on the couch, drink some wine, and drunk text Patrick."

"Oh God, please don't. I don't need to walk in on *that* again." There were definite drawbacks to having a roommate, and coming home to find someone blindfolded and draped over a chair was certainly one of them.

Wrapping up about six more chicken nuggets into a napkin,

Micki said good-bye and walked out of the school, feeling as if she'd just been sprung for the day. She waggled her fingers sweetly in a sarcastic wave to Savannah, who was pulling out of the parking lot in her jet-black Infiniti. Savannah didn't wave back.

CHAPTER TWO

Micki sat at her desk in the bullpen of the police station. Normally, the chief would have an office, but the only office in the building was under remodel. The fact that it had been that way since Micki'd been appointed chief didn't go unnoticed. The construction was moving at a snail's pace, and knowing Savannah, were it any other project in the town, it would have been completed approximately thirteen months earlier, around the same time Savannah had hired the crew to do the work. But every time Micki brought it up, Savannah would shoot her right down. She'd make her feel selfish and egocentric for even suggesting that her office take precedence over a wheelchair-accessible ramp at the high school or a playground outside the community daycare. So, Micki just shut her mouth and sat next to Jack and Billy in the white-walled bullpen. At least their computers had been upgraded to technology that had been released in the 2000s.

"Yes, Mom," Micki said, toying with the coiled phone cord. "I don't see what the big deal is. Having a roommate doesn't bother me, and Rebecca is great. Yes, I know I'm the chief of police, but have you googled what the chief of a town like this makes? I don't live in San Francisco. Okay. I didn't think I would have a roommate at thirty either, but what can you do?" She pinched the bridge of her nose, exhausted by the conversation they had every time she called. "They just brought in a serial killer; I have to go. I'll call you later. Tell Dad I love him. Bye."

Micki sighed dramatically and looked toward the ceiling. She knew her mother meant well, but it was draining to have to defend her career and her living situation over and over again. Though she might have envisioned herself storming through windows for the SWAT team at one time, even Micki was surprised to find that she was perfectly content exactly where she was.

"I hope I don't have a roommate at thirty," Billy said, smirking.

Micki peeked at his monitor and saw he was playing one of those seek-and-find games that takes place in a detective's office. Fitting.

"Really?" Micki asked, raising her eyebrows.

"What? It's on-the-job-training. I should get a bonus for this."

"You're *definitely* going to have a roommate at thirty. Your mom."

Billy scoffed but laughed anyway. He was used to being ribbed for his age. The only three employees of the Winter Valley Police were Billy, who'd graduated high school three years earlier; Micki, the chief; and Jack, who didn't ever let on what his real age was. Could have been sixty, could have been ninety. Only Micki knew, since she had to provide his annual reviews, but she was happy to keep his secret.

"TM was in here earlier looking for the public safety budget proposal," Billy said, not looking up from his screen. Random visits from the town manager were never a good thing.

"Shit, why? She said it had to be in by the end of the day." Micki checked her watch. "It's only four o'clock. That gives me eight hours to finish it."

"Sure, Mick."

"I bet she hasn't hassled the fire department for *their* budget proposal yet," Micki muttered. She sharpened a pencil down to a nub.

"I didn't have to, Chief Blake. Chief Patel had his budget on my desk yesterday."

Micki closed her eyes as the raspy, biting voice of the esteemed town manager filled the bullpen. "Yes, Ms. Castillo. Chief Patel is a shining star of public service, and I am a walking example of what *not* to do." Micki didn't bother to turn around, knowing full well it would irk Savannah.

"As long as we're on the same page. I need your proposal no later than six tonight. Email it to me. I have to start reviewing them, and yours takes a *very* long time to weed through."

"Yes, ma'am," Micki said through gritted teeth and started sharpening another pencil down to its nub.

"Good night, Officer Parker," Savannah said to Billy, and her heels clicked as she walked back out of the station.

"Good night, Ms. Castillo!" Billy called out loudly.

Micki glared at him. "Traitor." She pulled out the stack of half-completed forms and requests and sifted through them. Micki wished that Billy or Jack could take on some of the administrative duties, but neither of them had shown any kind of predisposition toward them in her admittedly half-assed training session earlier that year. Jack had nodded off a few times, and Billy had seemed to find his fingernails fascinating. What she really wanted was that admin person she'd been routinely denied.

Pushing the paperwork to the side, Micki scrolled through the 9-1-1 database to see if anything interesting had come in. Nothing. She checked her appointment schedule. A meeting with Parks and Rec on Thursday at nine a.m. She refreshed her in-box. *Twenty percent off all ankle-length socks. Hurry, sale only lasts twenty-four hours!* She looked back to the messy scatter of forms and checked her watch.

"Fine," she grumbled and pulled up last quarter's spreadsheet.

CHAPTER THREE

Third one this week! Someone definitely has a secret admirer," Chloe said, raising her eyebrow playfully.

Savannah cast a glance at the coffee table in her office, the unwanted gifts lying in a messy pile. "What is it this time?" Savannah asked, sighing in frustration.

"Not sure. It's wrapped." Chloe gently placed the box on Savannah's desk. There was no return label, and the only identifying mark on the package was the word "Savannah" scrawled in sprawling calligraphy.

Savannah first eyed Chloe, who was smiling gleefully, and then the nondescript package. She had hired Chloe against her better judgment. The need for an assistant won out over the glum reality of a consistently chipper presence in the office. Chipper wasn't really Savannah's thing.

"If they're too cowardly to identify themselves, then why should I bother opening it?" Savannah brushed the box aside and began flipping through the papers on her desk.

"Aw, come on, don't you find it the least bit romantic? Someone has a crush on you from afar and is working up the nerve to tell you." Chloe gestured toward the wilting flowers and heart-shaped box.

"No. In fact, I find it quite trite. Flowers? Candy? When

was the last time you saw me eat a truffle? Exactly. Never. This *admirer* clearly doesn't know me in the least."

"Just open it. If it's another bust, I'll throw it all out, and we never have to speak of this again," Chloe said, smiling with her head cocked.

Savannah drummed her fingers. Chloe was getting very comfortable very fast. She wasn't sure how to feel about it. The perky little redhead didn't seem to treat her with the same apprehension she had come to expect from nearly everyone. Over time, Savannah had come to appreciate the control her standoffishness had afforded her, but she had to admit, she didn't completely *hate* that someone seemed interested in her as a person. "Fine," Savannah said sullenly, tearing the brown paper off the box. She used scissors to slit the tape at the top, and they both jumped when something sprang out at them.

A battered jack-in-the-box, caked with what appeared to be years of dirt and mildew, swayed haphazardly on its rusted spring. Its eyes had been removed, leaving only the hollowed-out circles where they once had been. Savannah backed up quickly, knocking her chair into the wall.

"This one's not so romantic," Chloe said as the head creaked eerily back and forth. She tugged at the corner of notebook paper sticking up behind the toy. "I don't get it."

"It's obviously someone's idea of a sick joke. And it's not particularly funny. What does the note say?" Savannah asked, her hand on her hip. At first, there was the tiniest bit of flattery associated with the attention. But unpredictability wasn't something Savannah embraced. So, by the time the second item had arrived, she was over it. Now she was definitely irritated.

As Chloe unfolded the bulky paper, her eyes grew wide. The plastic eyes that had been removed from the jack-in-the-box were glued to the white page, with only three words written below in the same scrawl as the package.

"I'm watching you," Chloe read, holding the paper out to Savannah. "Well, this just took a creepy turn."

Savannah scoffed. "I know there are plenty of people who don't like me. I'm sure someone is having a laugh at my expense. It's nothing," she said, though she knew her voice lacked conviction, and she hated the feeling of being out of control.

"I don't think you should ignore this, Savannah. We should do something."

"And what do you suggest we do? Plan a stakeout? Rig a booby trap?"

Chloe ignored her sarcasm. "I think we should call the chief."

Savannah would rather eat pasta with a thumbtack. "We will do no such thing. That woman is an imbecile. I'd have better luck with a stakeout."

"Certainly no disrespect, but Micki's actually quite good at her job. I know you two have had your differences, but—"

Savannah interrupted with a well-placed "Ha!" a tad louder than she had meant to.

Again, Chloe ignored her. "*But* she has experience with this kind of thing. I mean, she was basically a private eye before coming to Winter Valley. And what does a private eye do for a living? They stalk people professionally. So, I'm sure she knows what to look for in a stalking case."

"Chloe." Savannah wasn't about to let this become something more than a stupid prank. She refused to give a foolish jokester that type of credence. "Please do not refer to this as stalking. Someone is trying to scare me. That's all. And it won't work, I assure you." She flipped her hair and straightened her back, hoping she looked more confident than she felt.

"Can we just run it by her? Maybe you're right. Maybe she'll think it's nothing." Chloe stared at the creepy toy with distaste. "I just think we're better safe than sorry on this one."

"While I appreciate your concern, Chloe, there is no 'we' in this situation. I'm a grown woman, and I can handle this on my own. Please dispose of this," Savannah said in disgust, motioning toward the jack-in-the-box.

At Savannah's nod, Chloe took the offending items in her arms and closed Savannah's door behind her.

Savannah let out a deep sigh once Chloe had finally left the office. She rationalized that what she had said was true—she did have a fair number of people who disliked her, even if it was on a surface level. Mostly disgruntled politicians, scorned employees, and others who just didn't care for her. Savannah didn't care about that; she never had. Winter Valley was where she had finally hung her hat, but before she had settled in the small town to raise her daughter, she'd worked in political positions throughout New England, and she'd been damn good at it. She'd worked hard to get to where she was. And she didn't do it by being soft. Her obligations in this world didn't include coddling others. She was blunt; she was direct; she was straightforward. She was fair. Most of the time.

As much as it pained her to admit it, this latest gift was more than a little unsettling. The flowers and candy and other assorted gifts were just silliness. She paid no attention to those things. But this one…this one had a message. And Savannah didn't appreciate it.

❖

Oblivious to the world around her, Micki weeded through the folder of parking tickets, one of the most lucrative violations in the town. Somehow, it seemed fitting that the majority of the tickets came from restricted spaces in front of Town Hall. She startled when a box was unceremoniously dumped onto her yellowed blotter.

"Chloe! What the hell? What is all this?" Micki asked, moving her cup of coffee to the other side of the mess.

"I'm here on the down-low, Mick. Don't tell anyone."

"Anyone meaning a certain brunette? About yea tall? Generally unpleasant?"

Chloe rolled her eyes. "Yes."

Micki sighed. "So, what is all this?" She poked at the jack-in-the-box with a pencil, grimacing.

"First of all, I know Savannah acts like she has control over everything and everyone, but this is not one of those things. I can't ignore the pit in my stomach. I mean, I thought it was a little odd for someone to send the town manager this stuff, but this is like something out of a horror movie." Chloe pursed her lips.

"Whoa, slow down. What's been happening?"

"Savannah's been getting…gifts, I guess, over the last few weeks. They weren't obvious at first. Someone left a peach on her desk with a smiley face sticker on it. Of course, she immediately threw it in the trash. There was a basket of cookies with a ribbon tied around it. Again, right in the trash, but that could have been anyone. One of the new planning board members she hired, trying to suck up. We don't have the office locked up all the time, and I'm not always at my desk, so really, anyone. Then there was this pen and pencil set. This week, she received the flowers and a box of candy. Then today, this." Chloe curled her lip as she pointed to the damaged toy.

Micki frowned. "Yeah, this is weird. This isn't normal secret admirer behavior, if there even is such a thing. In this day and age, that sort of attention isn't usually welcome. But this…thing…has *threat* written all over it."

"There was a note, too." Chloe handed it to her.

Micki's eyes widened. "Oh, okay, yeah. She's being stalked."

"She doesn't like that word."

Micki looked up. "What? What do you mean?"

"She thinks it's someone just trying to have some fun at her expense. She doesn't want to make a big deal out of it, and when I suggested calling the police, she was adamant that she didn't want to."

"Of course she was." Micki bit her lip distractedly. "This only happens at her office?"

"As far as I know, yes. She hasn't mentioned anything about packages being left at her house, thankfully. Especially with Eliana there."

"Eliana. Yeah, she needs to take this seriously. I'll talk to her," Micki said, lifting a wilted rose with an ancient letter opener. Eliana, Savannah's seven-year-old daughter, was one of the coolest kids Micki had ever met. She loved to talk about comic books and video games and 80s movies. Strange that a child so easygoing could have been raised by a woman with the warmth of an iceberg in January.

"So, did you miss the part where I said you couldn't tell anyone?"

"How I am I supposed to investigate this if the *subject* doesn't know that I'm investigating? I have questions!"

"She'll kill me! Maybe not *kill* me but definitely fire me! I love this job," Chloe pleaded, clasping her hands together. "I'm on thin ice half the time anyway, but it's so much better than driving an hour each way into the city. Can't you just, you know, watch the building but not say anything?"

"So, basically stalk her to see who is stalking her, is what you're saying."

Chloe raised her hands. "Come on, Micki. What if it really is nothing? She'll be so pissed at me."

"It's *not* nothing. Even if it is someone who doesn't mean her *physical* harm, this still falls squarely into suspiciously threatening territory." At Chloe's crestfallen expression, Micki conceded. "I'll keep an eye on the office tonight, okay? I won't say anything. Yet."

"Thank you!" Chloe leaned in and hugged her. "I don't want her hurt, obviously, but I also don't want to get canned."

"I get it. Do the two of you get along now? I thought she was bitchy to you, too."

"I don't think we'll ever be best buddies or anything, but I've seen flashes of humanity in there, I promise. She even has a sense of humor, if you can believe it. Dry and biting, but it exists.

She's snide and derisive and crusty, but yeah, I guess I sort of like her now. When we're talking about her daughter or about the town, she comes off like a real person. Borderline caring and understanding. For real," Chloe said.

Micki realized she must have looked like a caricature of disbelief. "That's certainly news to me. But okay, go back to work. I'll deal with this," Micki said, motioning to her door. She snapped on a rubber glove and began to inspect the jack-in-the-box.

She frowned, looking at the evidence as a whole. It had started out innocently enough, with small tokens of affection. But then this. Was it because they hadn't gotten a response with the other items? Micki didn't necessarily like Savannah, but she didn't wish her ill either. She'd worked a few stalking cases as a PI in Providence, and in her experience, it was never simply misguided emotions. There was always more to it than that. And it was never good.

Working on something a little meatier than an illicit Rollerblader in Dr. Marvin's parking lot was exhilarating, but Micki almost felt as if she was out of practice. She quickly scanned her mind for the very few citizens of Winter Valley who frequented the lone jail cell, but none of them seemed likely. This was too personal.

Micki thought back to her last case in Providence, where she'd exposed a woman blackmailing her ex-husband for thousands of dollars a week. He'd been involved in an elaborate money laundering operation, and both of them were looking at serious jail time. Micki remembered the adrenaline, the fast pace of her legwork, the information forming a perfect puzzle. Did she miss it? Maybe a little. Would she go back? Not a chance.

The head of the toy creaked back and forth on its hinges while Micki examined the bottom for any identifying marks.

❖

Savannah stood at her full-length window, her dark-rimmed glasses dangling from her index finger. She was still bothered by the "present" she had made light of in front of Chloe earlier. If she hadn't fostered such an adversarial relationship with Deputy Chief Mackenzie Blake, she would have brought the box straight down to the station. But she didn't feel as if she could. Maybe there were times when she could have eased up on Chief Blake, but she had waltzed into town with her sweet nature and easygoing attitude, and it set Savannah on edge from the moment they met. She just didn't trust that anyone could be that genuine. Those people didn't exist. Everyone had an agenda, and although Micki hadn't shown hers yet, she'd turn out to be like everyone else. Even so, Savannah knew that Mackenzie would take the situation seriously if she brought it to her and look into it, but then Savannah would be at her mercy. She would appear weak. And that was something Savannah simply refused to do.

Savannah rejected any notion that her demand for order and control stemmed from anything other than her own self-confidence. And it had paid off. Her career was on track, the town was at ease, and her daughter was everything she could have hoped for. Savannah cast a glance at the framed photo of her daughter on her desk, Eliana about three years old and drinking from a garden hose. She smiled softly at the memory. Savannah vowed to make sure Eliana never questioned her own self-worth. She was enough. She would always be enough.

People walked back and forth beneath her window. The tiny town of 1,433 people at last count felt even more claustrophobic than usual. Savannah didn't see anything out of the ordinary or anyone who looked suspicious. She liked to think she'd honed her skills for spotting those who were sly or devious. She'd started wide-eyed and filled with excitement when she began her congressional internship after college, but the game had left her jaded and cynical over the years. Her first run for city council, in a midsize city in central Massachusetts, had given her a taste of the cutthroat nature of people. Savannah had been painted as a naïve little rich girl who would only work for the upper-class neighborhoods, who was only interested in helping the elite. She'd been shocked and angry, but she didn't know how to combat the lies. She'd lost that election by a wide margin. That night, surrounded by a cockeyed banner that read "Savannah for Southbridge" and what supporters she had left, Savannah decided the only way to win was to strike first. Always strike first. She sighed and sat back down at her desk, determined not to let a game of cat and mouse rattle her. Since the phantom toying with her didn't have a physical form yet, she had no one she could strike first. She'd just have to ignore them and hope they'd go away.

CHAPTER FOUR

The windowsill hadn't been cleaned in…maybe never. Micki grabbed a wad of toilet paper and grimaced at the smear of dirt and dead bugs as she dropped it into the wastebasket. She looked across the alleyway that separated the town hall from the police station and raised her binoculars. It was a limited vantage point, but she had a decent view of the front and side of the building. Savannah's Infiniti was parked in its usual reserved spot, a tiny orange cone placed on either side of the painted lines. Micki rolled her eyes.

The first time Micki saw Savannah Castillo, after dropping off some paperwork for the town council soon after she got to Winter Valley, she was exiting the elevator in the freshly painted town hall building. Micki's breath had caught in her throat.

Savannah had sauntered past her, owning the air around her. Her shoulder-length chestnut hair flipped up slightly at the ends, her expensive, form-fitting black dress screamed class, and her shiny pumps accentuated perfect calves of rich bronze. Micki was fairly certain she had given Savannah a cartoony, wide-eyed once-over, which resulted in an immediate blush. She had tried to look away but found she couldn't.

Things only continued to escalate from there.

"Can I help you?" Savannah had asked, sounding amused.

"No!" Micki had answered, much too quickly. "Definitely not. All set here."

"Mmm." Savannah had adjusted her sunglasses before heading toward the front door. "It's a Valentino."

"What?"

"My dress. You seemed to be staring, so I assumed you were interested in the designer?"

Micki nodded furiously, her face flushing hot. "Yes, thank you. I'll write that down. Do you happen to have, um, a piece of paper? Or maybe a pen?" She'd looked toward the reception desk. When she turned back toward Savannah, she saw only the back of her through the glass of the revolving door. Micki looked down at her own outfit, a faded Red Sox T-shirt, ripped jeans, and her comfy Crocs sandals. She closed her eyes in embarrassment. There was no way that woman thought Micki was interested in the designer of her dress.

Nope.

That was probably the height of their relationship and one of the only encounters that hadn't ended in ugliness. Micki wasn't a stupid woman. She knew why Savannah didn't like her or at least what had set her off in that direction. Micki hadn't realized that voicing her opinion at a town meeting would turn into a grudge-laden feud with one of the most powerful women in the town. Otherwise, she might have just kept her opinion to herself.

When Savannah had purchased a landmark building right after Micki joined the police force, one member of the board had wanted to launch an investigation into the legality of Savannah's real estate acquisition. Micki had supported the opposition to Savannah's team tearing down the Winter Valley Quilt Museum to make way for a car dealership. She felt it would detract from the small-town feel that most people seemed to love so much.

Savannah's lawyers were able to make the whole thing go away before an investigation could even get off the ground. There was no evidence of any wrongdoing, and she was able to move forward with the purchase. Savannah and her team had decided to leave the museum intact.

So, what was the problem? Micki's assumption was that that would be the end of it. She didn't see any particular reason that they couldn't just let bygones be bygones and move forward professionally.

Savannah provided her with reasons. Many, *many* reasons. Jack had warned Micki about voicing opposition to the TM, as embarrassing her in a public forum was a surefire way to make a lifelong enemy out of her. He'd suggested that she speak with the mayor privately, but Micki had brushed him off. Savannah was a big girl, and she could surely understand that people had differing opinions. Apparently, Jack had been right. It was all in the delivery.

Savannah's wrath persisted when the former police chief retired and the town council appointed Micki to the position. Savannah had backed the résumé she'd received from a candidate from Manchester for the position. He was a decorated police officer with years of service behind him. Micki could understand why Savannah had been apprehensive about Micki taking the position, but she *didn't* know why Savannah seemed to have taken it so personally. Sure, she'd only been a police officer in town for a short time, but it wasn't her first foray into law enforcement. And in a town the size of Winter Valley, there wasn't a whole lot of crime to deal with. Besides, she was good at her job. Everyone knew it. Except Savannah Castillo.

Micki didn't understand all the politics that went on behind the scenes, and she sincerely didn't want to. She'd been sure that Savannah would somehow veto her appointment, but for whatever reason, that hadn't happened. Maybe she didn't have the authority. But she sure liked to make it seem as if Micki owed her a debt of gratitude every time she sat down at her desk.

Savannah had made it a point to attend all town council meetings regardless of the minutia of the agenda or the necessity of her presence. She continually made counterpoints to everything Micki suggested and corrected her at the slightest misstep. Attendance skyrocketed when word got out that Savannah routinely tried to embarrass the new police chief. It became something of an event. Word on the street was that she viewed it as payback for the failed real estate venture and being overridden in the chief appointment. Things had always seemed to go Savannah's way before Micki had come to town.

Earlier that fall, Micki had suggested a carnival in town to raise money for flood victims after a terrible storm in the south.

"So, this might seem like a lot of work, but it'll definitely be worth it. We just need some volunteers to get us started. Here are a few sign-up sheets," she'd said, passing around the paper and pen. "Lots of positions available. Creating fliers, selling tickets, setting up booths, finding a DJ, food vendors. All kinds of things."

"We could do that." Savannah's voice was loud at the far end of the table. "Or we could invite Cody Pratt to perform on the common."

There were audible gasps in the conference room.

"How would we manage that? He's the hottest singer in the country right now. There's no way he'd come to Winter Valley for free," one of the councilmen said, resting his folded hands on his belly.

"Oh, he's already offered. I know his father quite well and explained exactly what we were trying to raise money for. The whole family will be in Vermont on a ski weekend next month, and Cody's more than happy to help us out."

"That's amazing!" someone yelled from the back of the room.

"My daughter is going to freak out!"

The councilwoman holding the volunteer sheet for the carnival tore it in half. "We'll raise triple the money with Cody Pratt coming to town, and we won't have to spend anything on booths or vendors!"

Micki had smiled through gritted teeth. "That's wonderful, Savannah. Thank you." She sat back down in her chair, deflated and annoyed. Anything to steal her thunder. Literally, *anything.* Yeah, it had been a good idea. But why not combine it with Micki's? It hadn't even been a discussion.

Micki was well aware that Savannah thought she was inept. Mostly, it didn't bother her. When it came down to it, Savannah ran the town well, and Micki respected her for it. The few times that Savannah had seemed to forget about their rivalry, their thought processes were very similar, and their goals were comparable. Then Savannah would remember that Micki had pissed her off that one time, and her airs would come right back. They just weren't going to get along. There was no way around it. Micki could either suck it up and work around it or quit. And she was no quitter.

CHAPTER FIVE

Steam rose from the mashed potatoes Savannah doled out onto two plates. Eliana sat in anticipation, her fork and knife held tightly between two small fists.

"Extra butter?" she asked hopefully.

"Just enough."

Eliana's face fell but quickly perked up at her first bite. Her mom's mashed potatoes made having to eat the disgusting boiled asparagus worth it.

After a few moments of companionable silence while they ate, Eliana took a long sip of her apple juice. "Micki loved my egg-carton-flower-bouquet."

Savannah's mood darkened, but she tried to maintain a neutral expression. "When did you see her, Eliana?"

"This afternoon. She stopped in to pick up her sunglasses."

Savannah blanched. Eliana hadn't mentioned anything about an art project to her. "Would you like to show it to me?"

The fact that Micki lived in the same apartment as her daughter's babysitter sent flames up the side of Savannah's face. That she felt the need to ingratiate herself into every facet of Savannah's life enraged her. Imagined or not.

Eliana motioned toward her backpack, hanging on the hook in the front hall. "It's in there." She shrugged.

Savannah shoved a forkful of asparagus into her mouth to

disguise the hurt. "I assume that Chief Blake has a lot of work to do, and she probably doesn't need a first grader monopolizing all of her time. Did you finish all of your homework?"

"I don't see her every day," Eliana said, sullen. "She's super nice, you know. She told me that…"

Savannah listened and nodded in the right places, trying to look engaged. It took effort since her favorite time of day with her daughter was now tainted. She knew she was overreacting, but she was beginning to feel like a prisoner in her own town. A self-inflicted issue, sure, but a prisoner nonetheless. "You know, Mrs. Lawson at the doctor's office has mentioned that she does child care as well. Maybe it would be good for us to try something new?"

"No!" Eliana whined. "I don't want to go to Mrs. Lawson's after school. I like going to Rebecca's."

"That's fine, Eliana, it was just a suggestion."

Rebecca wasn't exactly Savannah's favorite person in the world, but she'd always been wonderful with her daughter. Savannah couldn't justify pulling her daughter out of Rebecca's care just because she didn't particularly like her roommate. Savannah didn't particularly like very many people. She'd grown up happy, sheltered. But then the people she'd trusted most had either let her down or died, so the branches on her olive tree no longer extended very far.

They finished in near silence, dinnerware clinking and ice tinkling. Eliana trudged up the stairs to do her mother-required nightly reading. Savannah brought the dishes to the sink, clanging the silverware loudly against the stainless steel. Taking out her disappointment on the cutlery was childish but satisfying. Disappointment in herself, mostly. She gripped the edge of the sink with both hands, hanging her head in defeat. She'd never doubted her abilities as a mother. Not ever. But lately, she felt as if she was letting Eliana down again and again. She tried, she really tried. Eliana was spontaneous and fun-loving and exciting. And Savannah was…not. It tore her apart to think that Eliana would rather spend her time with Rebecca and Micki than her. Maybe she should buy a pair of roller skates. That would be spontaneous, right?

Flecks of remorse for the way she treated Micki would pop up now and then, but something like this would happen, and even though it wasn't Micki's fault, the silent rage would begin to boil again.

The shrill ding of the doorbell startled Savannah out of her reverie. She wiped her hands primly on the dish towel near the sink and made her way to the front door, her heels clicking loudly in the otherwise quiet foyer. She pulled it open expectantly.

"Hello?" she called cautiously over the empty stoop, fear beginning to rear its head.

No one there. No answer.

"Who's there?" she called again. She expected silence at that point and received exactly that.

Savannah slammed the door shut, flipped her dead bolt, and fastened the chain. She felt hot tears spring to her eyes. *Who is doing this*, she thought, fighting a chill. Why *are they doing this?* She brushed the hair out of her face and strengthened her resolve. No one was going to intimidate her. *No one.* She went into each of the downstairs rooms and double-checked the locks on every window. She turned on the floodlights to illuminate the backyard. The branches from her weeping willow tree cast an eerie shadow on the stone patio. Savannah closed her eyes, pushing away the paranoia that was rapidly threatening to take over.

As she finally began to feel satisfied that the house was safe, she heard a light knock on the front door. She froze, waiting to see if it was actually a knock or just the flag, a branch, a fucking earthquake. Anything else.

The knock repeated, louder this time. Savannah jumped, inhaling deeply.

"Mom?" Eliana called from upstairs. "Is someone at the door?"

"No," she called back, wiping her cheek rapidly. "It's just the wind."

She looked out the beveled glass of the front door and didn't see anyone. What she really wanted to do was call the police. But her stubbornness, her absolute *defiance* wouldn't let her. *How sad I am*, she thought and chuckled bitterly. *It's nothing. If there were a real threat to me or to Eliana, I would swallow my pride and call the police. But I won't allow myself to get swallowed into a sick game.*

Gathering her composure, she unchained the bolt and snicked the door open softly. Unsurprisingly, there was no one there. She did, however, see an envelope lying on the top step. She shook her head, willing her heart to beat a normal rhythm again. It was just an envelope. Nothing could jump out at her from there.

She closed the door tightly after picking up the unaddressed envelope. She held it between her thumb and index finger as if it might bite. Savannah swallowed hard and ripped the edge off, shaking its contents into her hand.

On a lined 8.5 x 11 sheet of white notebook paper, a beautiful cursive penned the words:

> *Do you ever get the feeling you're being watched? I've read that it's a part of your brain that senses something is out of place, even though your conscious mind isn't registering it. It's not foolproof and certainly doesn't mean that someone is really there. Everything is usually fine.*
>
> *P.S. Asparagus is always better steamed.*

Savannah caught a sob in her throat before it escaped and slid down the front door, her back grinding softly against the smooth wood. The letter lay at her feet while she covered her face with her hands.

CHAPTER SIX

Micki raced into the small town hall auditorium, plowing through the doors just as the council members were finishing the recitation of the Pledge of Allegiance. The five sets of eyes at the council table whipped away from the flag and toward her to see what the commotion was.

"Sorry," she whispered sheepishly, slapping her hand over her heart.

Once they finished roll call and pushed past the regulatory town business, Micki cautiously raised her hand. Everyone turned to look at her. She always felt so stupid at these things.

One of the selectmen acknowledged her. "Deputy Chief Blake."

"I would like to request a full-time administrative assistant for the police department. In the past, this has been denied, but I believe we would be more effective as a department if we could delegate some of the more clerical tasks."

"As I've addressed with you in the past, Deputy Chief Blake," Savannah began, adjusting her glasses, "we have a strict board policy to keep budget increases at two percent or less. We do not have the room to add a full-time employee at this stage."

One of the council members spoke up, a woman who'd lived in town her whole life. She was Micki's best chance. "Ms.

Castillo, do we have the capacity to add *any* additional staff to the police department at this time?"

Savannah turned to her, hands folded in front of her. She smiled sweetly. She reached for a calculator and flipped to a specific page in her packet. "We could afford you ten hours per week of administrative assistance, Deputy Chief. Will that be sufficient?"

Of course not, Micki thought. Ten hours a week was nothing. "Well, Ms. Castillo, I'm not sure that amount of time will achieve the desired detraction from our current workload."

"We do need to stick to the budget, Deputy Chief," the councilwoman said, giving her a sympathetic look. "It's a fair compromise, don't you think?"

Savannah grinned at Micki.

"Sure," Micki said bitingly. "We'll take what we can get, I suppose."

After a quick tally of hands, Savannah removed her glasses and folded them in front of her. "Motion carried. Congratulations, Deputy Chief Blake."

Micki smiled, trying desperately not to look as pinched as she felt. *God, she sucks.* Did she *need* a clerical person? Probably not. They had time on their hands as it was. But Jack would be retiring soon, and administrative organization was one of Micki's admitted weaknesses. She was confident in her police work, but she didn't want incomplete or incorrect forms to underscore Savannah's perception that she wasn't good at her job. Shaking her head, Micki sat back in her chair and waited for the meeting to adjourn.

❖

"Could it be a pissed-off employee?" Micki asked, tossing a handful of fluorescent yellow popcorn into her mouth.

Chloe shrugged. "Maybe. But she's a pretty fair boss. At least in the time I've been working there. I've heard that the admin who was there before me had a crush on her, but that's it. Nothing else that I can think of."

"Well, yeah. That doesn't surprise me. If you can pretend she doesn't have the personality she does, she's a total catch. Maybe someone was trying to grease her palms, get her to do something, and she refused?"

Supernova, the one and only pub in Winter Valley, was unusually busy for a weeknight, but it gave Micki and Chloe the privacy they needed to talk about Savannah. No one could possibly listen in to their conversation; they could barely hear themselves over the loud twang of the country band up on the stage.

"You really think that's it?" Chloe asked, sipping her bright blue cocktail.

"No, not really. It seems a little more personal than that, but I'm trying to cover every angle. I've been looking through old articles and public records to see if there was some kind of zoning issue or public scandal that Savannah had any involvement in, but I haven't come across anything." Micki leaned back in her seat, sighing heavily. She ran her hand through her hair. "I really need to talk to her, Chloe."

"Well, you can't." Chloe took another sip of her drink and cocked her head thoughtfully. "Not yet anyway. I'm hoping it all just stops, and the psycho got the scare he was looking for."

"Or she."

"I guess."

A good-looking guy in his late twenties approached their table. "Hey, ladies. My friend and I just found this place on our way home from a hike. Would you mind if we join you?"

Chloe batted her lashes at him while Micki smirked at her. Chloe was about five foot zero with dark gray eyes and a wild mess of strawberry-blond hair that framed her face like a lion's mane. She received a lot of attention from the locals in town, but this time the focus seemed to be on Micki.

"You have beautiful eyes," he said, looking directly at Micki. "I don't think I've ever seen that shade of blue before."

"Thank you. Unfortunately, my friend and I were discussing something pretty important, so if you don't mind, it's not really a good time."

"And she's into women, so later on won't be a good time either." Chloe smiled, mixing her drink with the two little straws sticking out of it. "But I'll come say hi before we leave."

The guy raised his eyebrows. He nodded reluctantly and walked back to his seat at the bar. His friend turned and waved to them.

"Nice, Chloe," Micki said. She shook her head. "I need to know more about Savannah's personal life. What can you tell me about her ex, David?"

Micki shoveled in another handful of popcorn and washed it down with a swallow of Coors Light.

Chloe shrugged again. "Not much, really. I don't know him very well. We were on the same human dogsled team last year at the winter festival. I think that was right before they split up. He was fine. Nice enough, I guess. They just didn't fit. She finally broke it off after deciding there just wasn't anything left between them."

Micki discreetly pulled a compact notebook from her back pocket. She grabbed a keno pencil from the table and scribbled furiously on her lap. "So, she left him. Good to know. Do you know how he took it? And how do you know this stuff, anyway?"

"The same way I know about everything. Small town. From what I've heard, David was pretty broken up about it."

"Also good to know."

"I don't think it's him, Mick. He's bland, not bonkers."

"It's always the quiet ones, Chloe," Micki muttered, making a final note before replacing the pencil into its plastic holder. "This is good, though. Keep thinking."

"Hey, girls." Rebecca slid in next to Chloe. "What are we talking about?"

"Stacey," Chloe said quickly. Micki shot her a dirty look.

Rebecca made a face. "Why? What about her? You don't miss her, do you?"

"No. Not really. That was almost a year ago. I mean, I'm pretty sure I'm destined to be alone, so that's cool." Micki picked at the label on her beer bottle.

"Oh, stop. Stacey was a flake, let's be real." Rebecca flagged down a waitress and ordered a glass of wine.

"Be nice. It wasn't her fault I was emotionally unavailable." Micki shrugged. "She wanted more; I was afraid to give it to her; she found someone who wasn't. Can't really blame her."

"She could have waited maybe a week, don't you think?" Chloe asked. "I know you weren't together *that* long, but still."

"Whatever. I hope she has a wonderful life. I just don't need to be a part of it. To Stacey," Micki said and raised her beer in a toast.

Chloe and Rebecca clinked glasses with her, but they both shook their heads. "You're so evolved," Rebecca said. "I think I'd *still* be sending her nasty texts if it had been me. Could be why I'm still single."

Micki chuckled. Her feelings about the Stacey situation really were dormant, but she wished Chloe had come up with something else to change the subject. Micki wasn't interested in combing through the details of their failed relationships. She really just wanted to talk about Savannah. Was she really the reason Savannah was so reluctant to involve the police? Something about that gave Micki a pit in her stomach. She'd never been someone's nemesis before. At least that she knew about. How could someone be that upset about a real estate deal or a job assignment? It just didn't make sense. There had to be more to it.

Shrugging off her thoughts, Micki ordered another drink and tried to immerse herself in the conversation. If Savannah wanted to handle things on her own, then let her.

❖

Savannah stood in line at Cuppa Joe's, checking her watch repeatedly. She'd barely gotten any sleep after the incident with the phantom door knocker. The bell above the door chimed behind her. She turned to see Micki and Rebecca walk in, both with sunglasses still covering their eyes. Savannah audibly tutted at their obvious hangover attire.

"Ooh, that cheddar bagel looks good," Micki said. Her voice sounded deeper than usual. "Is it the last one?"

"Maybe. I'm just getting a coffee. The thought of cream cheese makes me want to yak." Rebecca shivered dramatically.

"Not me. I want the chive cream cheese to go with it. Delish."

Savannah leaned forward. "Joe?"

"Yes, ma'am, just finishing up your cappuccino."

"Thank you. Do you have any more cheddar bagels out back?"

"Sorry, Ms. Castillo, that's the last one."

"Okay, I'll take it to go, please."

Joe wrapped up the last cheddar bagel in a wax paper bag and handed it to Savannah. She smiled brightly at a dumbstruck Micki on her way out of the shop.

"Did she really?" Savannah heard Micki ask Rebecca.

Rebecca couldn't stifle her laugh. "She really did. Maybe it was a coincidence."

"Oh, please. She just didn't want me to have it. No surprise. Maybe they still have onion bagels or something. I was just really in the mood."

Savannah's satisfaction faded. When had she become so petty? She wouldn't stand for her daughter to behave this way; why should she? With her hand on the door handle, the bell chimed weakly at her hesitance. She turned around and walked toward Micki with purpose.

"I just remembered that I have still have leftover coffee cake from yesterday's meeting in my office. Here," she offered, holding out the bag.

"Oh," Micki said, taking the bag gingerly. "Thank you. Let me pay you for it."

She started digging in her pocket for cash, but Savannah was already walking away. She hurried out the door, not wanting to overhear any more of their conversation. They'd probably ask if the Grinch's heart had grown three sizes that day, or maybe they'd laugh because she had backed down from her spitefulness in a show of fragility. Either way, she didn't want to hear it. Maybe she'd start asking Chloe to pick up her breakfast.

CHAPTER SEVEN

There's been another one, Mick," Chloe whispered into the phone. "I found it sitting on the coffee table in the lobby. I don't know how this person keeps coming in here without anyone noticing. I asked Bobby in permits and Jane in zoning, and neither one of them saw anything out of the ordinary."

"And of course, she denied our bid for surveillance technology in the municipal buildings last quarter," Micki muttered. "Okay, so what is it?"

"A snow globe. It's a sun setting on a mountain, and it says 'The Sunshine of Pikes Peak' on the front."

Micki frowned. "Pikes Peak? Where's that? Does it mean anything to her?"

"Yep. She was visibly freaked out when I brought it in to her. She wouldn't admit it, of course, but I could tell. She said Pikes Peak was the last place she went on vacation with her parents before her father died. She's been wanting to take Eliana there for a while now. How freaking creepy is *that*?"

"Very." Micki sighed. "Does she know that you told me yet?"

"No! I brought it up again today, and she was like, 'We're not doing that.' And then she asked me to get the parks department on the phone. I think it was just her way of getting me out of her office."

"This is stupid, Chloe! Then tell her to call Jack or Billy! They're police officers, too!" Was Savannah really so stubborn she'd put her safety at risk? Did she really dislike Micki so much she'd rather be a victim?

"Yeah, right. I'll try, but you know she won't go for it. Maybe I can talk her into hiring a PI. We have to do *something*, though."

"This isn't stopping or just going away like you'd hoped. I'll see what I can find out, but this is making my job much harder than it needs to be when I could just *ask her the questions*." Micki threw her pen down on her desk and watched in horror as it exploded blue ink all over the scattered documents.

"I know. Just a little longer. Maybe that was their final 'gift.' Something sweet and insane all at the same time."

"Maybe. But I doubt it."

Micki hung up and stood. She'd decided to let Savannah deal with it on her own, not wanting to insert herself where she wasn't wanted. But she was beginning to feel as if she had to do *something*. Sitting around waiting for someone to make a move, a potentially dangerous one, wasn't in Micki's blood. If Savannah was too obstinate to realize she needed help, then that wasn't Micki's problem. If something happened to her or her daughter, then that certainly *was* Micki's problem. And it wasn't something she was about to let happen.

From below her balcony, Savannah heard the crunching of gravel. She immediately went to her bedroom window, separating the blinds with her index finger just enough to see through the sliver of darkness. She squinted for a better view and could just make out something outside. There was a car parked underneath a tree across the street, obscured by the neighbor's stockade fence. Savannah saw the light of a phone turn on for the briefest of seconds, and then the car was again in blackness.

She checked on Eliana for the fourth or fifth time, and thankfully, nothing had changed. She was sound asleep in her bed, the steady hum of the ceiling fan providing the only background noise. The snow globe weighed heavily on Savannah's mind. She racked her brain to remember who in her past knew that story. She supposed she'd shared it with those she had grown close to over the years, but she could remember no specifics. *That's what you get for opening up to people.*

She went back to her bedroom window and saw that the car was still parked in the same spot. She couldn't make out any details such as make or model, but she strained her eyes just the same. Her eyes widened as the motion light at the neighbor's house went on and off in brief succession as someone inside let their cat in. The quick illumination didn't show much, but it did show the outline of a 90s-era Crown Victoria.

Savannah gasped. Fire filled her as she bounded down the stairs and threw her front door open. As she stormed across the street, her bare feet didn't even register the cold of the asphalt or the pebbles that pierced her skin. She could almost hear the Wicked Witch's theme song accompanying her fervor. She made her to way to the window of the car and banged on it furiously.

Micki's eyes widened, and her mouth dropped as she opened the car door. She stepped out furtively, holding both of her hands up in an act of submission.

"Savannah, I—"

She was interrupted by the crack of Savannah's palm slamming into the side of her face, causing her to stumble backward. Her hand went to her lip, which was now coated with red.

"You think this is funny?" Savannah screamed at her, hysterical with rage. "How could you do this? I'll have you removed from the force before the blood on your mouth dries! Why are you doing this to me?" she yelled, bringing her hand up again for a second blow.

Micki regained herself quickly, stilling Savannah's hand with a firm grip. "Hey, whoa! It's not me, Savannah! I'm only trying to—"

"Okay, you win, you fucking psychopath! You scared the hell out of me! You reduced me to—"

"Savannah!" Micki yelled and looked around as if she was wondering if the neighbors were going to start streaming out of their houses to investigate the commotion. "Chloe told me."

Savannah stopped short. She stared at Micki for a moment. She closed her eyes, trying to regain control.

Micki spoke fast. "I was watching the house. I am *so* sorry. I didn't mean to frighten you. I figured if someone was going to do something or leave something at your house, it would be in the middle of the night. She told me that you didn't want to involve the police—"

"I didn't want to involve *you*."

Micki ignored her. "So, I took it upon myself to see if I could figure this out. I don't want you or Eliana to feel threatened. I was trying to catch whoever is doing this in the act. Please, Savannah, I really am sorry. I'm only trying to help, I promise."

The anger began to filter away slowly as Savannah let out a long-held breath. "I knew I shouldn't have trusted her."

"Don't be mad at Chloe. She was just worried about you. Really worried." Micki swiped at her lip again, smearing the fresh droplets of blood. "And I think she's right to be. This could be serious."

Micki placed a hand on Savannah's arm until Savannah looked pointedly at it. Micki snatched it away. "Has there been anything else? I know about the little gifts and the jack-in-the-box and about the snow globe that was left today."

Savannah hesitated, but the cat was out of the bag, so to speak. There wasn't much point in staying quiet now. "Yes. A letter was left at my front door."

"When?" Micki asked.

"Last night. I don't know, maybe seven."

"Okay, now that you know I *am* involved, I really need to talk to you. I know it's the middle of the night, but I'd like to see the note, and I'd like to ask you some questions while the answers are still fresh in your mind." Micki shifted her weight at Savannah's non-response. "Um, please?"

Savannah gave a half-hearted shrug and started back to her house. Her large gray colonial was bathed in darkness except for a soft light coming from her bedroom window. At least Eliana had slept through the drama.

A reluctant wave of relief swept through Savannah. She hadn't asked for help because she hadn't wanted it. Or so she had told herself. But now, with Micki following behind her, maybe there was a small part of her that *didn't* want to go through this alone. For the first time since all of this had started, Savannah felt a shred of that suffocating isolation begin to dissipate.

She opened the door slowly, mindful of Eliana sleeping upstairs. It had been a while since they'd had company other than one of Eliana's school friends over for a playdate. She breathed deeply while Micki closed the door behind them.

CHAPTER EIGHT

"Wipe your feet," Savannah commanded, not even bothering to look back.

Rolling her eyes, Micki sheepishly scuffed her boots on the rubber mat, kicking off nonexistent dirt. She followed Savannah into her study where she took a seat on the plush leather love seat. Micki tried not to marvel at the perfected interior design and cleanliness of a house inhabited by a seven-year-old. It was pretty much exactly as she'd imagined Savannah's house would look. Micki wondered if there was a playroom somewhere that had crayon-covered walls and puzzle pieces littering the floor. Doubtful. She felt a quick dose of shame for the state of her own bedroom. She sank right into the sofa and leaned back.

Savannah cocked an eyebrow. Micki sensed Savannah's surprise at her apparent comfort level, which was, in reality, zero. She crossed and uncrossed her legs. She cleared her throat.

"So, when did this start, exactly?" she asked, taking her pad and pen out of her back pocket.

Savannah sighed audibly and went over to her mahogany bar. She poured two glasses of gin and handed one to Micki. "Before I answer any of your questions, what qualifies you to investigate this?" she asked, air-quoting the word "investigate."

Micki couldn't help her amusement. "I am the deputy chief of the Winter Valley Police Department." Duh.

Savannah scoffed. "Oh, you mean over the two patrolmen that you consider to be your employees? One of whom must be nearing ninety and the other who recently graduated high school? Have the three of you been setting Havahart traps for squirrels outside Cuppa Joe's?"

Micki's cheeks flushed with anger. "You know what? If you don't think I'm qualified, then fine. I'll step aside, and you can find someone else to deal with your bullshit." She stood up and put the untouched glass of gin on the coffee table.

"Two weeks ago."

"What?" She stopped and turned before she was out of the room.

"It started two weeks ago."

Micki watched as Savannah picked at a tiny thread on the side of her ottoman. She sighed and sat back down. "And what items were left for you?"

Savannah downed a good amount of gin. "Please, Chief Blake, my assistant must have filled you in on the gory details. No need to make me repeat them."

"Again, Savannah, she was just looking out for you. And I'd still like your perception of the things left for you. Can I see the letter?"

Huffing again, Savannah retrieved the letter from her desk and thrust it at Micki.

Annoyed by her frustration, Micki snapped at her. "Look, I'm sorry you're so put out by me asking questions, but your cooperation would *really* be appreciated. I'm just trying to do my job."

"Thank you *so much* for actually earning your salary," Savannah spat, her eyes flashing. She paused, seeming to have realized that she'd crossed a line. She put up a hand in surrender. "I'm sorry. I'm just frustrated."

Micki opened her mouth to reply and promptly closed it. She rubbed the back of her neck and opened the envelope. She sat quietly for a moment before changing her tone completely.

"This is serious, Savannah."

"I'm aware of that, Chief Blake."

"I've never seen someone escalate this quickly. First it was a few trinkets, then flowers, then that fucked-up jack-in-the-box, to now...spying on you in your home? That usually takes a few months, not days."

"I've always been an overachiever," Savannah said, downing the rest of her drink.

"Who might have a problem with you?"

Savannah laughed, running a hand through her hair. "I'm not sure there's enough time left before breakfast."

"Come on, I'm serious. Let's talk about David."

Savannah bristled. "It's not David."

"Okay," Micki said, smiling tight-lipped. It was like pulling teeth. "I still need to ask about him. How did your relationship end? Amicably? Was it one-sided?"

"Yes, it was amicable enough. I told him that I didn't see any real future for us, so it would be better if we went our separate ways. He disagreed, but I was firm in my decision."

"Was he upset?"

"I suppose he was."

"Did he ever lash out?"

Savannah flung herself backward dramatically into her high-backed chair. "No, *Micki*, he didn't. He called a few times, and that was that."

"Why are you so sure it isn't him?"

"He isn't the type. He's mellow. Placid."

Micki scribbled furiously. She wasn't certain that David should be ruled out just yet.

"Did he ever do anything that made you feel like he was dangerous? Or to suggest that he was having a hard time letting go?"

"Not particularly, no."

Savannah stood up to refill her glass. Micki couldn't help but notice her bare legs beneath the short robe she was wearing.

She shook her head to clear away feeling like a creepy lecher. This was business, and her focus needed to remain on that.

"Who else?"

"Your dear friend Rebecca has always disliked me. I'm sure she wasn't pleased with the professional nutrition guidelines that were sent over to the elementary school."

"What? She watches Eliana for you every day after school!"

"I didn't say she disliked Eliana. She dislikes *me*. I can put aside my differences for the good of my child. Rebecca is a very competent provider, and she treats Eliana well. That doesn't mean she wouldn't want to rattle me."

"Come *on*, Savannah, it's not Rebecca."

"Oh? How can you be so certain?" Savannah asked innocently, raising her eyebrows.

Micki smiled. "You know what? You're right. I'll look into Rebecca. In fact, I'll move her to the top of my list."

"Um…" Savannah tapped her finger to her chin repeatedly. "There's also…you."

Micki looked up quickly from her notebook, a mix of shock and hurt colliding in her chest. "Me? Savannah, I don't dislike you. I mean, you're a bitch to me more often than not, and you've tried to run me out of town and take my position away from me and poison the entire town against me, but *dislike* is a strong word."

Savannah smirked. "I think you've just uncovered motive."

Micki shook her head. "I don't like some of the things you've done, but that doesn't mean I don't like *you*. From what I've heard, you're an excellent mother, I know you run the town like a well-oiled machine, and when you're not actively being mean to me, you're sort of tolerable," Micki said, reflecting on the few times they'd interacted like actual human beings. They were far and few between, but there had been a *couple* of occasions. Maybe. "I think we need to focus mostly on romantic entanglements, based on the nature of the gifts. That includes people who have taken an interest in you or asked you out, and you declined. And obviously past and present relationships."

Savannah softened, though Micki could almost see her chastising herself for doing so. She cleared her throat. She didn't bother to thank Micki for damning her with faint praise. "There are no present relationships. My former assistant Jamie didn't leave on the best of terms. I had to fire him. He was becoming... inappropriate with me. But as far as I know, he moved out of state."

"Okay, that's a good lead. What happened?"

"He was an excellent assistant, really. Right on top of things. He bought me a gift under the pretense of office décor, which I absolutely loved. It's the mirror you see hanging in my lobby. In hindsight, I never should have accepted it. He'd make comments here and there that could have been misconstrued, but I chose to overlook them in favor of his skill. That was my mistake and one I won't make again. I should have cut the cord immediately."

"Has he reached out to you at all since his termination?"

"He's emailed a few times. A few of them were apologies; a few of them were looking for employer recommendations. I ignored them all."

"This is good. I want to look into him. Any other relationships to speak of?"

Savannah looked at the ceiling thoughtfully. "Only one, really. But I can't imagine her mustering up the motivation or having the patience for any kind of long game. Patience was never her strong suit."

Micki's head snapped up. "Her?"

"Yes, Chief Blake. *Her.* Do you have a problem with that?"

"No, of course not! No. No problem. Don't be silly." Micki scratched her forehead and looked back to her notebook. "Name?"

"Cori. Coriander Girard. She likes to tell people it's derived from a Mediterranean term for love. But her mother told me they named her that because they'd eaten chutney on the day she was born." Savannah's face was awash in something like amused nostalgia.

"Was it an antagonistic breakup?" Micki asked, trying desperately to will away the smirk that threatened to break through.

"No, not really," Savannah answered, stretching her legs. She seemed to have settled into something resembling a comfort level. "She was one of those clichéd wild spirits that just couldn't stay in one place for very long. If you *must* know, Chief Blake, she left me."

Micki nodded, not sure how to react to that. Sure, Savannah was uptight and snarky and condescending and a total snob and a little mean, but she was also *incredibly* beautiful. Looks certainly weren't everything, but in this case, Micki believed they could probably overcome quite a bit. Her train of thought had gotten derailed, *again*. She brought her attention back to Savannah's breakup.

"When was the last time you spoke to her?"

"It's been a while. We text now and again, usually quick messages like 'how are things' and 'thought of you today because of xyz,' but even that's been well over a month."

"How did you make your money, if you don't mind me asking? I assume it wasn't in your current position?" Knowing what the chief of police's budgeted salary was, Micki couldn't imagine town manager was a whole lot more.

"First of all, what makes you think I have money? And what does that have to do with anything?"

"Okay, well, it's no secret that you're wealthy. And while I do believe this is of a more personal nature, I just want to make sure I look at every angle. It could be a business deal of some kind in your past that didn't go well."

Savannah pursed her lips. "I've been successful with my real estate investments. I work alone, so there is no partner to consider. And I haven't evicted any orphanages, so you can strike *that* thought from your mind."

"Well, that's a relief. I did wonder about it. Have you thought about politics on a grander scale? Like, maybe heading up a town of five thousand instead of fourteen hundred?"

"No. I specifically sought out a town like this all those years ago. I wanted the intimacy and safety of a small town." Savannah scoffed. "Ironic."

"So, there's no one else that you can think of? No one else who's made you feel uncomfortable or vigorously pursued you? Nothing like that?"

"Chief, I'm a woman; of *course* I've felt uncomfortable. But, no, I can't think of anything else in particular."

Sometime around four o'clock, Micki yawned as she tucked her notebook safely back in her pocket. "This is good, Savannah. I have a lot to work with here. We'll find this crackpot, I promise." She stood, cricking her neck back and forth. "Do I have your permission to tell Rebecca what's going on? As Eliana's afterschool caregiver, I think she should know. She needs to be on alert for anything suspicious as well."

Savannah nodded, gathering up the glasses from the coffee table. "I suppose so. Although I can't even imagine them targeting Eliana. I don't think I could take it. Thank you, Chief Blake." She placed a tentative hand on Micki's upper arm. When she realized what she had done, she pulled it back as if she'd been burned. "I expect I'll hear from you with your results?"

"Yes, definitely," Micki said, her skin tingling from where Savannah's fingers had been a moment ago. It was probably just the shock of contact without some form of malice behind it. "Please, call me if anything else happens. If there's any new thing left for you, if you see anyone out of place, or even if you just *feel* like something is wrong. No chances." Micki tightened her jacket and opened the front door. "Promise?"

Savannah gave her the side-eye. "Yes, Chief Blake, I promise. I'll keep you abreast of my whereabouts at every moment."

Micki laughed awkwardly. "Okay, then. Tell Eliana I said hello. I'll talk to you later."

Savannah nodded politely and closed the door behind her.

Looking around her wearily, Micki walked to her car. She didn't notice anything out of place or see anything out of the ordinary. But the fact that someone was brazen enough to leave something on Savannah's front doorstep worried her, especially something that let Savannah know they'd been looking through the window. Getting caught didn't seem to be at the forefront of the offender's mind.

She unlocked the door and sat in her car for a minute, blowing on her hands as the Crown Vic's heat rattled to life. She didn't *really* dislike Savannah with any sort of deep-seated hatred. She was bitchy and cold, but Micki had always assumed that was just how she portrayed herself. Micki knew Savannah thought she was annoying and impulsive and out to oppose everything Savannah proposed, but that wasn't the case. She enjoyed poking the bear once in a while, but it was just a surface thing for Micki. Something about their whole exchange bothered her. Shrugging, Micki shifted her car into drive, feeling troubled and more than a little dejected. Though she couldn't seem to pinpoint exactly why.

❖

Savannah sat at her desk, the words on her monitor blurring together. She'd thought about taking a sick day after the previous night with Micki but ultimately decided that she would only sit around and brood. Sleep was no longer a reliable escape.

A knock on her door interrupted her haze, and Chloe walked in with a steaming cup of coffee. "I thought this might help," Chloe said, shamefaced, speaking low.

Savannah looked up and then immediately back down at her paperwork. "Thanks," she muttered. She still wasn't sure how to proceed with her assistant or, as she now liked to refer to her, the traitor. She knew Chloe was only trying to help, but the intrusion more felt like a breach of trust than a supportive SOS.

Chloe couldn't hold it in any longer. "I'm so sorry I told Micki but, Savannah, that thing was just so *creepy*, and I didn't want anything to—"

Savannah held her hand up. "Miss Rhodes, I had assumed this went without saying, but in light of recent events, I feel I must clarify. An executive assistant at this level is a position which *requires* confidentiality. There are many aspects of my position and yours that necessitate a tight lip. If you cannot meet those job requirements, please feel free to hand in your resignation."

Chloe's face fell. "Savannah, I would never break your confidence or put the office in jeopardy." At Savannah's quirked eyebrow, Chloe hurried to finish. "It's just, this particular situation could have a physically harmful effect on you, and I don't want that. Please understand, I wasn't doing it out of spite or to engage in any kind of gossip. I'm worried about you."

Against her will, Savannah could feel the anger toward her assistant begin to diminish. She sighed dramatically. "I didn't want the police chief involved for personal reasons. That may have been the wrong approach, I'll admit. But if you ever betray my trust again, Chloe, we'll move to immediate termination. Is that clear?"

Chloe nodded furiously. "Yes. I really am sorry. I'm just scared."

"It's fine."

Savannah turned her attention back to her computer, silently dismissing Chloe from her office. Chloe took the cue and skulked out, closing the door gently behind her.

It still irritated her that she'd even allowed Chloe to know what was going on. Though it wasn't like there was anyone else Savannah could turn to, and Chloe had opened a few of the gifts and letters anyway. She'd kept herself isolated over the years, choosing career over relationships. There was uncontrollable risk letting someone in, but advancement in her career posed a risk that could be contained. Savannah's only real friend from her childhood was now a big oil executive and had temporarily moved to Siberia to oversee the latest mining expedition. When she returned in four or five years, she'd be set for life. Savannah wasn't sure that a text saying she was being stalked, oh, and how's the cold treating you, would be appropriate. Savannah's relationship with her mother had become strained over the years, and they rarely spoke. There was no one she could talk to. Savannah fought off the suffocation of that revelation and tried to focus on her spreadsheet.

Moments later, another knock interrupted Savannah's concentration. "Yes?" she asked bitingly, now thoroughly annoyed with emotions she didn't have time for.

"Sorry," Micki said, sheepishly removing her fuzzy hat. The early spring afternoon was raw and cold. "I just wanted to let you know that I'll be reaching out to Jamie and Cori today. According to his manager, David is in Jamaica. I've left him a message to contact me as soon as he returns. Crossing our t's and dotting our i's."

"Okay...is there something you would like me to do? Provide a heads-up courtesy call, perhaps?" She just couldn't help herself, and she winced internally at the sarcastic comeback. It was amazing anyone spoke to her at all, really.

Micki cleared her throat. "*No*, Savannah. I'm only telling you in case they reach out to you after the fact. That happens sometimes. If it does, please do not engage or answer any questions and refer them back to me."

Savannah nodded curtly. She paused. "This is embarrassing," she said quietly.

Micki sighed. Savannah watched as Micki gingerly walked over to her. She placed a hand lightly on her shoulder. Surprising herself, Savannah didn't pull away. "It shouldn't be," Micki said. "This isn't your fault; you did nothing to deserve this. It really has nothing to do with you. Whoever is doing this—this is their deficiency, or whatever, not yours."

Savannah swiveled in her chair, effectively removing

Micki's hand. The closeness was unnerving, more so because she found she wanted it. "Well," she said, all business. "I do know that, of course, in the abstract. But it doesn't feel that way, being the object of their...whatever this is."

"I know," Micki said, offering a tight-lipped smile and moving back toward the door. "I'll let you know what I find out."

Savannah nodded, startling at the sound of the door closing. She groaned at her constant edginess. She was beginning to come around to the idea that Micki might actually do a good job. She hadn't found anything yet, but she did seem genuinely concerned and intent on finding out who was doing this. Savannah had surprised herself by admitting that she found the whole situation embarrassing, but Micki had handled it with grace. Maybe even a touch of compassion. Savannah reached for her glasses and focused on her monitor, where the town motto splashed against her desktop. *Winter Valley: Where No One Is a Stranger.*

❖

It was odd, seeing Savannah in a new light. She was still as prickly and pompous as ever, but Micki was adept enough to see the brief flickers of humanity. Savannah was scared, and she was obviously struggling with what appeared to be an unfamiliar emotion.

Her hand resting on her head, Micki twirled the phone cord. "In your own words, please, why did your employment with Ms. Castillo come to an end?"

Jamie Gagnon scoffed. "I made the mistake of revealing my true feelings for her. Had she not been so convinced of our employee-employer stance, I'm certain she would have seen the value in me as a lover."

Micki swallowed the urge to vomit. "And then she let you go?"

"I was persistent, I will admit. I very innocently tried to

rid her of stress late one evening by a tried-and-true massage technique, and that was when she told me that she 'no longer required my services,' I think was how she put it."

"So, you harassed her." Micki cringed, knowing she shouldn't be setting a suspect on the defense, but she couldn't help herself.

"I did no such thing, Chief Blake."

"Right, okay. Can you confirm your whereabouts last night?"

"I was at home. I made a lovely chicken piccata and watched *The Bachelor* on television."

"And you're still living in Middletown? I assume you live alone?" She couldn't imagine being anywhere near him, let alone living with him.

"Interesting assumption, Chief, but a correct one. Yes, I do live alone."

Micki looked toward the drop ceiling, examining the scattered brown trails that hinted at water damage from long ago. "So, no one can confirm that you were in your apartment, or even in the state of Connecticut, last night between six p.m. and ten p.m.?"

"I did go to the market for some capers around five or six last evening."

"Excellent. Please provide me with the name of the store, and if you recall, the lane where you checked out or the clerk's name. Email me your receipt as well." Micki scribbled on her notepad, taking down the few details Jamie was able to provide. She didn't like this guy, but she didn't have any kind of gut reaction that he was the one she should be concentrating on. When he asked why she wanted the information she just thanked him for his time and hung up. She wasn't about to give him a reason to go knocking on Savannah's door in some kind of hero gesture. She shuffled paperwork aimlessly, unsure where to look next.

❖

There were few instances in her life when Savannah allowed her will to be broken. After the begging and pleading had become too much to handle, Savannah had relented. She was running on fumes, in a constant state of alert. Maybe it would be nice to have the house to herself for the night.

Rebecca had invited Eliana to sleep over at her house since Micki's nine-year-old niece from Concord was visiting. They'd have a fun girls' night sleepover, with movies and popcorn and games and pizza. Savannah wasn't pleased that Eliana was in the room when Rebecca had made the suggestion, which made it impossible to say no outright. Since then, of course, Eliana could speak of nothing else. And when Eliana came out with a suitcase bursting with clothes and her favorite teddy sticking out, Savannah couldn't help but smile. She didn't always allow for a whole lot of fun in their house, and that was something she'd have to work on.

When Rebecca had come to pick her up, with Micki and her niece in tow, Savannah answered the door wordlessly. She smiled at the young girl and turned toward the two women. She nodded her greeting.

"Hey," Micki said, standing just over the threshold in the foyer. She whispered, "This wasn't my idea. I know with everything going on, this probably doesn't seem like the best time for a super-fun sleepover. If you don't want her to come, I can explain it to Riley. She'll be cool about it."

For some reason, Savannah was inclined to believe her. Micki had been acting differently toward her. Kinder, gentler. Savannah knew that it was probably born of pity, but she had too many other things on her mind to fully contemplate *that* particular shade of humiliation.

"No, Eliana's been looking forward to this. I haven't seen her this excited in a long time, so I won't take that away from her." Eliana bounded down the stairs, calling a joyful hello to her awaiting carpool. Savannah shoved Eliana's overnight bag into Micki's chest. "Have fun. Eat sensibly." Eliana and Micki smirked at each other in silent resistance.

Micki held up her hand as Savannah waved to her daughter from the front porch, absentmindedly checking her mailbox before closing the door behind her. Micki felt somewhat reluctant to leave, though Savannah hadn't given her much of a choice. Confusion danced within her temples. Savannah was a big girl who didn't need a babysitter. So why did Micki feel as if she needed to be there with her? Probably just leftover creeps from her earlier conversation with Jamie.

Rebecca flipped on the radio in her Camry, and the girls in the back seat danced along to a Kidz Bop version of a Katy Perry song. She looked over at Micki.

"What's wrong?"

Micki stared out her window, her chin resting on the back of her hand. "Nothing. I don't know. I feel bad leaving her alone."

"Why? I can't imagine a seven-year-old would be much help if something happened anyway."

Micki nodded. "I know, it's stupid. I can't even imagine. I mean, what if they took her? Or she woke up, and her mother was missing? Or *worse*?"

Rebecca put a finger to her lips, but the girls in the back seat were oblivious, talking animatedly about dalmatian puppies.

"Do you really think it's that bad? You don't think it's just someone trying to get under Savannah's skin?"

"I don't know." Micki shrugged, shaking her head. "My gut tells me it's more than that, but I hope I'm wrong. I just feel bad. I wish she was coming with us."

"Okay, that's weird. You hate her."

"I don't *hate* her. Jeez." She glanced over her shoulder to make sure the girls still weren't paying attention. She wouldn't want Eliana to hear that kind of thing.

"I'm pretty sure you do." Rebecca laughed. "What was it again? Uh, Dragon Lady, Torture Queen, Her Royal Bitchiness…"

"Okay, okay," Micki said, grimacing. She put her hand up. "Am I really that immature?"

"Yep."

"Well, I shouldn't have said those things. I'm sorry."

"Why are you apologizing to me?"

"I don't know; it felt like the right thing to do." Micki paused. "Hey, girls, who wants to pick up some frappes on the way home?"

Eliana and Riley cheered as Rebecca pulled into the Dairy Do.

Micki turned her thoughts to chocolate or coffee, since dwelling on the idea of Savannah alone in her house was making her stomach turn. She needed to switch her mind off, and Eliana's demand for a game of blindfolded Twister when they got home was probably exactly what she needed.

CHAPTER NINE

By ten o'clock, Savannah was ready to call it a night. She did her now nightly walkthrough, checking all the doors and windows before going to the bathroom to brush her teeth. Her eyes stared back at her, tired and fatigued. The house was quiet. She'd just snuggled into her heavy down comforter when she realized she'd left her book in the study.

She sighed heavily and padded down the stairs, only to stop short on the bottom step. The rapid shift in momentum nearly made her stumble.

Her front door was cracked open.

Savannah tried to make a sound, but her throat was constricted. A primal fear she was unfamiliar with made her dizzy, and she gripped the stair rail tightly.

She walked slowly toward the door, raking her mind for the possibility that she had left it ajar when Eliana and Micki had left hours earlier. She knew in her heart that it wasn't true, but for sanity's sake, she reasoned with herself that it must have been. If someone was in her house, she would know. Wouldn't she?

She closed the door and entered her study, slowly and quietly. It was empty. She reached for the fire poker and clutched it so tightly that her hand would bear the marks of the wrought iron design for hours. Savannah could feel tears form behind her eyes, but she refused to let them fall.

"You Are My Sunshine" suddenly blasted from the kitchen, so loud that the speakers were crackling, so loud that Savannah couldn't hear the sob that escaped from her throat.

She started to run toward the front door, poker in hand, and found that it was open once again. She screamed, unable to justify that all it would do is reveal her location, and turned away from the door, thinking the intruder could be standing right there, waiting.

The music continued to assault all of Savannah's senses. She tried covering her ears, but it was futile.

As the song continued, she ran toward the stairs, blind with fear, reason forgotten, moving forward on instinct alone.

She made it to her bedroom, where she slammed the door and locked it, her hands shaking so profusely that it took her three times to push the button in properly. From the kitchen, she could still hear the blasting music, now only slightly muffled.

In a momentary flash of unmitigated relief, Savannah spotted her cell phone on the edge of her nightstand. She stumbled over to it, falling to her knees. She texted Micki with trembling hands.

He is in the house. Please come now. Please help me.

The speakers continued to blare the happy tune, creating chaos within the terror that cloaked her. Savannah covered her ears again, crying openly. She looked at her phone to see the text message bubbles appear, then immediately disappear.

I'm coming.

Savannah wept in a stomach-turning mix of relief and terror.

Thank God she's not here. Savannah allowed herself a moment of gratitude that her daughter was at a sleepover instead of being traumatized by the monster in her house. The music continued to play, the song set to repeat, while Savannah waited the longest six minutes of her life, curled against her bed with her knees drawn up to her chest, the fire poker still firmly in her grip.

❖

Micki screeched to a halt in front of Savannah's house, her tires leaving tread marks on Kensington Road. She jumped out of her car, not bothering to close the door. She leapt onto the front stoop, ignoring the steps completely. The door was cracked open.

She quickly unholstered her standard-issue Glock 22, the weapon she favored when she was off duty, holding it tightly near her shoulder with both hands. Micki kicked the door open the rest of the way, momentarily confused by the blaring music. She checked the hallway and study, her heart beating rapidly. She made her way to the kitchen, where Savannah's Bluetooth speakers were bursting to capacity. She pressed the pause button with her knuckle and turned with her weapon pointed straight ahead of her, thankful that the racket was no longer pulsating through her ears.

The downstairs was clear.

Micki made her way upstairs, her back against the wall as she listened for signs of commotion. She was grateful that she didn't hear anything, but her anxiety began to grow as what the silence *could* mean began to infiltrate. She pleaded with any higher power listening that she wasn't too late.

She confirmed every room upstairs was empty, including Eliana's, before finally making her way to the only closed door on the upper floor. She turned the knob, and it didn't budge. She couldn't risk calling out and letting the intruder know she was there if he was, in fact, in the room.

Micki backed up a step, raising her booted foot toward the door. She lunged forward, adrenaline giving her super-strength. The door slammed loudly against the wall.

She saw Savannah sitting against the bed, making a move to stand. Micki put her hand up to stop her. "Are you alone?" she asked as she gently eased the closet door open. Nothing.

"Yes," Savannah whispered.

Micki made her way to the attached bathroom, where she violently pushed aside the shower curtain with her gun drawn. Empty.

Feeling moderately confident that no one was in the house any longer, Micki holstered her pistol and rushed over to where Savannah was still sitting immobile.

"Are you okay?" she asked quietly, kneeling down next to her, kicking the fire poker away.

"What kind of a stupid question is that?" Savannah spat, tears beginning to spill down her cheeks. "Do I look okay?" Despite her words, Savannah reached out, her arms circling tightly around Micki's neck. She held on to her and cried.

Still rigid, Micki's eyes widened at the uncharacteristic show of vulnerability. Cautiously, Micki wrapped her arms around Savannah's waist, and she rested her chin on her shoulder. For a brief moment, she closed her eyes and inhaled Savannah's unmistakable scent. Lavender mixed with something heady, like musk. It was a little bit like heaven.

"I got here as quickly as I could." Micki gently rubbed Savannah's back in wide circles.

"I know. Thank you for coming."

Micki nodded into her shoulder, unsure what to say. Of course she came. She was angry at herself for leaving at all earlier that evening. She'd had a feeling something was off, and she'd ignored it.

"I don't know how he got in," Savannah said, pulling back from the embrace. She wiped at her eyes. "I know I locked the door, Micki. I know I did."

"I'm sure that you did. We don't know how long this person has been watching you. Maybe they did something to the locks or found another way in. I'll have the locks changed this week. We'll figure it out, I promise," Micki said, reaching out again and brushing Savannah's dark hair away from her face. Touching her was sort of…nice.

"I can't live like this. Maybe I should go away for a while. Take Eliana and just leave." Savannah looked up at Micki with wide eyes glittering with tears from a seemingly endless well that she probably didn't even realize existed.

Micki shook her head emphatically. "That is the complete opposite of what you should do. We can't let them win. Eliana needs safety and stability; the town needs you here to ensure things continue to run smoothly. *I* need you here," Micki said without thinking. At Savannah's look, she quickly clawed back. "Without your input, we'll never find this guy."

Savannah sighed and nodded reluctantly.

"The force doesn't have the resources for twenty-four seven surveillance, which you're aware of. The bureaucratic bullshit needs to stop when it comes to the town's safety. Obviously, we don't have to get into that right this minute." Savannah glared at her. "But as of right now, we officially have the resources again," Micki said, nodding in affirmation to her own statement.

"No, Chief, you don't. You and the two deputies are really all we have, aside from the citizen volunteers. And I don't particularly trust anyone right now."

"Yes, we do. We do because I'm going to stay with you. Until all of this blows over, until we arrest and incarcerate this motherfucker, I'm going to stay here. You have more than enough room, don't you?"

Savannah looked at her with a mix of shock and disbelief. "I believe that is *highly* inappropriate, Chief—"

"I don't really care, Savannah. This guy was in your house. That puts you and your daughter in serious danger."

Savannah hesitated. Micki waited for her to fight with her, scoff at her, laugh, something. Nothing came except a soft sigh.

"Fine. Will you be gathering fingerprints? Taking plaster molds of shoe prints?"

It was Micki's turn to be surprised, but she tried not to show it. She had expected much more resistance to the idea. Even though it was spur of the moment, she was frantically reassuring herself that it was, in fact, a good idea.

"Well, again, we don't have those kinds of resources. I'll definitely use the kit we have at the station, but I wouldn't expect much from it. My assumption is that they wore gloves. Clearly, you watch way too much *CSI*. Was the song that was playing 'You Are My Sunshine'?"

Savannah's lip curled in disgust. "Yes, it was. It sounded like a little girl's or maybe a little boy's voice. I don't know. Used to be one of my favorite songs to sing to Eliana when she was younger. I guess that's it for *those* particular memories."

"I agree. The little kid version of it just added to the weirdness. I'll have to check it out tomorrow to see if it's just a random song or if there might be any significance to it. Cross check it against the items that they left."

Savannah shot up. "Is the front door still open? He could have come back in!"

"No, no, I locked it once I had cleared the downstairs. I wanted to make sure they couldn't just sneak out while I was looking around."

Savannah's shoulders relaxed. She breathed deeply in and out, coming down from the abysmal high. Then she gave Micki the once-over. "Exactly *what* are you wearing?"

Micki looked down at her clothes and blushed. "Look, I didn't have time to get my uniform on, okay? I jumped out of bed!" She had on black and white plaid flannel pants and an oversized T-shirt that read in faded block letters *New Kids on the Block.*

"I didn't realize you enjoyed 'Hangin' Tough.'" Savannah smiled in spite of herself.

"I got stuck with it at a Yankee swap a few years ago," Micki mumbled. "It's comfortable!"

"Well, don't take it personally. I mean, you've obviously got 'The Right Stuff.'"

"Oh, fuck off, Savannah." Micki chuckled, torn between hugging her and strangling her. "Eliana is with Rebecca and Riley tonight, so she's fine. I'll shoot Rebecca a quick text to let her know that you're okay and that I'll be staying here."

"Tonight?"

"Yes?"

Secrets in a Small Town

Savannah nodded. "Okay. That's fine. And, Micki, don't worry. We'll just take it 'Step by Step.'"

Micki smiled and shook her head. "You're a riot. Who knew? Anyway, can we get some sleep? I'll do another house check, and then I *really* need to crash. We have a lot of work to do tomorrow. Should I just take Eliana's room?"

Savannah's face fell, and her eyes clouded with worry. "Yes. That's fine."

"Are you sure?" Micki asked, sensing her hesitation. "Do you want me to sleep in here?"

"You don't need to make *everything* into an enlightening course in humiliation, do you? I'm just...a little on edge at the moment."

"Savannah, it's fine, really. I'll just grab some blankets and pillows and find a comfy spot on the floor."

The thought of sharing Savannah's bed with her was both terrifying and exhilarating, but Micki didn't want to seem presumptuous. Three days ago, the woman was spitting venom at her.

Silent for a moment, Savannah nodded. "Yes, thank you. Micki?" she said as Micki was leaving the room. "I do appreciate this. I'm not always the best at expressing gratitude, but...thank you. Really. Thank you."

"You're welcome," Micki said, a grin slowly taking shape. "It'll be like our very own sleepover. I haven't had one of those since I was a kid."

Savannah pursed her lips, her mask falling back into place. "And you're not having one now. This is definitely *not* like a sleepover."

"You ruin everything." Micki laughed. She winked at Savannah and began to check and double-check each room in the house.

• 75 •

CHAPTER TEN

Early morning light streamed through the windows, rousing Savannah from her restless slumber. Her fear had finally subsided a little, thanks to Micki, but her mind wandered back to someone in *her* house, touching *her* things, violating *her* safety. She hoped it would all just go away, that they would lose interest, but something inside told her they weren't satisfied. That maybe they never would be. But she knew she couldn't live like that. She slowly opened her eyes and leaned over the side of her bed. She saw Micki curled up in a ball, Eliana's purple princess comforter covering all but her eyes.

An unfamiliar feeling washed over Savannah, gratitude mixed with…something else. Fondness? Affection? She shook her head to rid herself of such silliness and used her toes to gently nudge Micki awake. She was just doing her job. Maybe she was a better police officer than Savannah had given her credit for. It obviously wasn't commonplace behavior to sleep on a victim's floor, but Savannah could easily enough chalk it up to small-town solidarity. Even if they *did* loathe each other. For the most part.

Savannah smiled as Micki grunted and pulled the blanket completely over her head. She nudged her again.

"I don't know what you do in your own home, Chief Blake, but in this one, we actually get up at a reasonable hour."

Grunting again. "What time is it?" Micki asked, her voice full and throaty.

"Seven."

"Seven! In what world is that a reasonable hour?"

"I have to take Eliana to soccer practice. We don't just lie around like sloths all day." Savannah couldn't hide her amusement at the deputy chief of police using a princess comforter to shield herself from the outside world. Micki groaned and stuffed her head under the pillow. Savannah wondered if she should snap a quick photo.

"What time is soccer practice?"

"Nine."

"Nine! It's seven! I can have another hour, *at least.*"

Savannah continued to poke her with her foot until Micki threw the covers off of herself dramatically. "I'm up, I'm up." She scratched her eyebrow, her hair wild and mussed. "I have to go get my stuff. You coming?" she muttered.

"Your stuff?"

"Yes, my *stuff*. If I'm going to stay here for a while, I'd like to have some of my own things. Is that okay with you? I promise I won't let my plebian possessions come into contact with your pristine palace."

Savannah rolled her eyes. "I'm not sure I understand why I need to be there?"

"Well, you don't, but I need to go pick up Riley, and I thought you might like to get Eliana? I'd like to be there when you tell Eliana I'm staying with you. She knows you hate me, so I want to see her expression. She'll think you've lost your mind."

"I don't hate you, Micki," Savannah said quietly. That hurt. She'd never been anything but caustic toward Mickey, so there was no reason to expect anything different. Still, she couldn't ignore the pang in her stomach.

Micki cleared her throat. "I guess I sort of know that now, but *she* doesn't."

Savannah tilted her head, looking at Micki curiously. "Won't your roommate have something to say about this?"

"I don't actually report to her. I'm allowed to stay out on school nights. So, come on, brush your teeth, paint your nails, drink the blood of a virgin. Do whatever it is you normally do in the mornings, but hurry up." Micki quickly folded the blankets into a messy pile and left them on the foot of Savannah's bed.

"Who said it has to be a virgin?" Savannah asked, raising an eyebrow.

"Funny. Hurry up."

Savannah smiled again, grabbing her purse off her dresser. She heard Micki clanging around in the bathroom and felt the tiniest hint of relief that she'd be there again that night. She was unnerved once again by her acceptance of Micki's offer to stay with them, but rather than analyze it, she rushed downstairs to collect cleats and kneepads.

❖

Eliana sat at the island counter eating a bowl of wheat flakes. Riley sat next to her, flipping through one of those catalogs that sells a thousand rubber ducks for a dollar fifty. Rebecca was sipping her coffee when Micki opened the door, Savannah in tow.

"Hey! So, what happened last night? I got your text but you…" Rebecca trailed off when she saw Savannah standing in the doorway. Savannah stood rigid, her hands shoved firmly into the pockets of her coat.

"Micki! *Mom?*" Eliana blurted out what Rebecca was obviously thinking. "What are you doing here?"

Riley looked at each of them in succession, clearly trying to figure out exactly what was going on. A blanket of disquiet hung over the kitchen. Everyone looked a little apprehensive. Micki coughed, trying to divert the awkwardness.

"Picking you up. You have soccer practice this morning."

"How come you came here together?" Eliana looked at her mother and then at Micki.

"If you can believe it, I'm actually going to stay at *your* house for a few nights. Cool, huh?" Micki thought she would enjoy the shock of Rebecca and Eliana finding out, but experiencing Savannah's discomfort wasn't nearly as enjoyable as Micki had imagined. She could almost feel the tension seeping out of her.

"What?" Eliana asked.

"What?" Riley asked.

"*What?*" Rebecca asked, her eyes the size of Easter eggs. She'd been tying her light brown hair back into a messy bun but let it fall back down on her shoulders. She just stood there, holding the black rubber band with her mouth open.

Savannah stepped forward, looking like she was ready to do battle. "Rebecca, I hardly—"

Micki lightly put her hand on Savannah's shoulder to stop her in her tracks. It worked. "Beck, I'll call you later after I take Riley home. I'm sorry to cut the visit short, honey. Something's come up, but I promise we'll do it again soon. I'll call your dad and explain everything on the way." Riley nodded. "And, Eliana, I'm sure you know that there's been some weird stuff going on in the neighborhood lately."

"Yeah, that's why my mom told me I had to turn on the ceiling fan instead of opening my window when my room got too hot the other night. Because of the weird stuff."

"Right. Exactly. So, until we figure out what's going on, I'm just going to hang out with you and your mom. Not that your mom isn't strong or can't protect you on her own, but sometimes it's nice to have another adult in the house."

"*Protect* us?" Eliana asked, her eyes filling with fear.

"Look, there's nothing for you to be afraid of! It's probably just somebody doing bad things to get attention. But I'm on it, and you know Jack? From the police station? Well, he's on it, too. We'll put a stop to this bad guy before you know it."

"Mom says Jack is a hundred years old and wouldn't be able to stop a baby from drawing on a wall."

Micki shot Savannah a dirty look. "Well, that's not true, Eliana. Jack is an excellent police officer."

Eliana acquiesced, but she didn't look entirely comforted.

"El, if you don't want Micki to stay with us—" Savannah began, but she couldn't get the words out before Eliana interrupted.

"No, I do! I do! We can play video games and eat ice cream and play Barbies in the living room!"

"Well, *no*, but I'm sure we can set aside some time for fun. Micki, why don't you help the girls get their things together?" Savannah asked, turning her attention to Rebecca.

Micki tried to speak up, but Rebecca cut her off. "Great idea. Savannah can help me clean up."

Riley and Eliana dragged Micki out of the kitchen by her sleeves, though Micki looked back at them with a frown. Neither acknowledged her.

When they were out of view, it was Rebecca who spoke first. "Savannah, what is your endgame here? I know you don't like Micki, you don't like Eliana spending time with her, and now you're asking her to *move in* with you? Is this some kind of long con to get her out of Winter Valley? To get her fired as police chief?"

Savannah was taken aback by her directness but not surprised by the content. "Actually, Rebecca, you've misjudged me, as you usually do. Chief Blake may not be as idiotic as I once thought her to be, though she can still be quite infuriating." Savannah cleared her throat to rid herself of the lilt in her voice and the smirk she couldn't contain. "However, it was not my idea for her to stay with me. I'm not sure exactly how much you know about what's going on, but it's...unpleasant, to say the least."

"Yes, Micki told me what was happening. I'm sorry. It's awful that someone is doing this to you."

Savannah nodded curtly and continued. "Chief Blake thought it would be in my best interest, and Eliana's, if she stayed at the house until this whole thing goes away. Last night was the most terrifying night of my life. I am quite grateful that the chief came so quickly and was able to chase the boogeyman away." With the way things were going, Savannah wondered if she should just call in to a radio show and tell the world what was happening to her and how it was making her feel. First Micki, now Rebecca. Savannah checked her sleeve to make sure her heart wasn't pinned to it.

Rebecca clearly didn't know how to respond. She'd been watching Eliana after school since kindergarten, but the only exchanges they'd shared were confined to lists, expectations, and reports that involved Eliana. She looked at Savannah skeptically.

"I know you think I'm a monster. I assure you, Rebecca, in this case, I am not."

Rebecca swallowed. "I don't think you're a monster."

"Don't. I've overheard you with some of the mothers at school. Do you remember El's autumn talent show? Casually saying how bad you felt for my daughter, that she had to grow up with an ice queen like me for a mother? I would have made a scene, but I didn't want to upset Eliana. So, I left. My point is, I know how you feel about me."

Pink crept up Rebecca's cheeks as she crossed her arms. There was no way out of that one. "I admit, that was childish and petty. I'm sorry, and I don't actually believe that to be true. I wouldn't be your child care provider if I didn't think you were a good mother or neglected Eliana in any way. You'd reprimanded me that morning for letting Eliana watch *Family Guy*. Which, in my defense, is a cartoon, so who knew it would be so crass? Anyway, I was angry and engaged in that kind of talk when I shouldn't have."

"I appreciate that. But that doesn't mean it didn't hurt."

Rebecca visibly recoiled. "You're right, it doesn't. I really am sorry."

Micki and the two girls emerged from the living room where blankets and pillows were still scattered on the floor. She had a black duffel bag slung over her shoulder and a canvas bag filled with junk food. Fritos and Smartfood stuck out of the top. Savannah eyed the bag suspiciously.

"What?" Micki asked. "I can't be expected to subsist on spinach and low-fat yogurt, can I?"

Eliana smiled broadly at her mother.

Savannah shook her head but didn't say anything. They thanked Rebecca for the sleepover and headed down the stairs of the apartment building. The worn red carpet had seen better days, but the exposed brick added some old-world charm to the place.

"See you tonight, kiddo," Micki said to Eliana, waving as Savannah confirmed that her seat belt was buckled tightly. She met Savannah's eyes when she stood up. "You, too."

Savannah just nodded.

"Let's go, Ri." Micki started her engine and flicked the switch so that the blue lights on the top of her car flashed. Riley laughed and called out a loud good-bye to Eliana from the passenger seat.

Savannah watched the cruiser pull out of the parking lot, the sun glinting on its fading taillights. The thought of Micki coming over after work, staying the night, created an alien knot in Savannah's stomach. There was so much about Micki that was exasperating, maddening even, but somehow, Savannah was unable to muster up the usual feelings of distaste toward her. She was appreciative. Maybe Savannah was just scared, and fear trumped just about every other emotion. Or maybe, after all these years, she was just going soft.

CHAPTER ELEVEN

As she sat on the sidelines of the soccer field, her legs crossed and her behind sore from the sagging canvas folding chair, Savannah looked at her phone repeatedly. One of her contacts, "Mom," was up on the screen, just waiting for the green dial button to be pressed. She continued to hesitate.

She hadn't talked to her mother in, what? Four, five months? They'd been close when Savannah was young. After her father died when she was just seventeen, their relationship began to slowly deteriorate. Her mother found fault in everything. No matter how much Savannah succeeded, there was always a gentle prod for how more could have been achieved, how it could have been just a little bit better. She'd gone from a caring, tender soul to a bitter widow who was angry at the world. And Savannah had receded right along with her into the uptight and controlling woman who'd pushed her away in the first place.

When Eliana was born, Savannah was sure that her mother would want to be heavily involved in her granddaughter's life. It had started out that way, but once her mom went back to Stowe, that was pretty much it. Savannah had asked her to move in with them, to stay for as long as she wanted to, but her mom declined. Said she had to get back to her daily life, her routine. She was president of the Rotary Club, and they simply couldn't get on without her. Savannah hadn't been close to her own grandparents when she was young, but that was because her *belo* and *bela* lived an ocean away. Her mother had always stressed the importance of extended family, but it never seemed to materialize in their lives. Savannah didn't know what it was like to be surrounded by grandparents and aunts and uncles and cousins in the way that so many Hispanic families were portrayed. Her family had been an island of three, and in the blink of an eye, an island of two. History had a funny way of repeating itself. Savannah had done her very best not to cry as she said good-bye to her mother, who was settling herself into the town car, preparing to go back to her solitary life. The baby on her shoulder had slept through it all.

In a moment of weakness, Savannah hit the call button. She put the phone to her ear and chewed on her lip. *Calling your mother shouldn't be this nerve-wracking.*

"Hi, Mom," she said when the call was finally answered.

"Hello, Savi. It's good to hear from you. I can't even remember the last time you called. How have you been?"

Savannah found it effortless to slip back into Spanish, something her mother had always encouraged. Savannah's father couldn't speak it, so it had become a sort of secret code between Savannah and her mother She'd promised herself she'd teach Eliana to be bilingual, but so far, she was falling short. Eliana only knew a few sentences at most.

She decided to look past her mother's signature passive-aggressiveness. "It has been a while. Sorry about that. Everything is fine."

"And Eliana?"

"She's fine, too." Savannah heard her voice crack and chastised herself. She was such a cliché. Hearing her mother's voice, no matter how long it had been, no matter how much distance between them, gave her the right to give up a little bit of the control she so longed for.

"Savi, you don't sound fine. Tell me what's wrong."

And that was it. The dam broke, and Savannah watched through a curtain of tears as her daughter chased fruitlessly after a soccer ball.

"I'm not fine, Mom. I'm not. Someone is after me, and I don't know why."

She told her everything, including the details of the Pikes Peak snow globe. Her mother gasped when she told her about it.

"Do you need me to come? I can rearrange some things here if I need to. I can come to you."

Savannah's heart filled. "No, Mom, you don't have to do that. The deputy chief is actually staying at my house for the next few nights until we can figure out who's doing this."

"Deputy chief? Like a security guard? Does every town manager get a security guard at their home?" Her mother was clearly confused.

"Well, no, not exactly. She's really—"

"She?"

"Yes, the deputy chief is a woman. She's really doing me a favor. When whoever it is showed up at my house last night, I panicked. And she came to my…" Savannah clenched her jaw. "Rescue."

"Okay. That sounds strange to me, but if she's willing to do that, I'm grateful. Savi, I know how you can be. You have to do everything yourself; you take help from no one. Don't do that. Let her help you. Don't be alone."

Savannah felt fresh tears spring to her eyes. For someone who cried once a year on average, she was breaking all sorts of records lately. "I know, Mom. I'll try. I don't want to be alone anymore. Not right now, anyway."

"Good. I'm going to come visit this summer for a few weeks. I'll let you know the dates when I've figured them out. I don't want us to be strangers. I'm tired of being alone, too. Your father wouldn't want this for us. You be careful, and you take care of that little angel."

Savannah nodded even though her mother couldn't see her. "I will, Mom. I'll call you when I know more."

"I love you, Savi."

"I love you, too."

"*Goal!*" someone screamed from the field. Savannah looked to the field hopefully, only to see a downtrodden Eliana standing inside the net with a ball rolling at her feet. She sighed and jogged over to the field to comfort her.

Eliana sucked in her bottom lip. "I couldn't stop it. I tried to kick it, but my foot went right over the top." She looked at Savannah expectantly. Savannah curled the end of Eliana's hair around her finger.

"So? Big deal. You'll get the next one. Or maybe you won't. Doing your best is more important than *being* the best. I will never expect more of you than your best. Eliana, do you have any idea how proud you make me? I don't care if you stop every goal that tries to come through or you never stop another goal in your life. You are enough."

Eliana smiled at Savannah. A girl on the other team yelled at her to throw the ball back in. "You have to get off the field, Mom! This is embarrassing!" But the look in her eye told Savannah that she was feeling something very different.

As she walked back to her chair, for the first time in a long time, Savannah felt as if she was the mother Eliana needed. Family was so important to Savannah's mother and father, and when her father died, Savannah's mother had let that part of her die, too. It had only been the three of them, since conceiving her had proven to be a lot more difficult than her parents had hoped. Her father had wanted a house full of children, but once Savannah had arrived, he'd told her that a hundred other children couldn't fill his heart the way she had. She'd never forgotten that, and she wanted to make damn sure Eliana felt as comforted by it as she had.

❖

"So, where should I put my stuff?" Micki asked, her duffel bag in hand.

Eliana came in behind her, holding the offensive canvas bag with all of the treats in it. She set it down and popped open a can of Pringles.

"Eliana, put those away. Dinner is in an hour." Savannah turned to Micki. "You can take the guest room next to Eliana's," she offered, starting toward the stairs. Micki followed.

This is really, really, *weird.* Micki felt as if she was spending the night at some great-aunt's house she had never met before, careful not to leave any footprints in the carpet.

Savannah led her to a nicely furnished bedroom. It was larger than Micki's own and a hell of a lot neater, too. The walls were a soft blue, and the bedding complemented it nicely with different hues of green. Micki nodded gratefully as she dropped her bags on the floor near the bed.

"TV?" she asked, scanning the room.

"No. But if you find it necessary, I can move the one from Eliana's playroom up here."

"Nope, that's okay. I should make the most of my ten bucks a month on Netflix anyway. Catch up on *Zombie Hunting* or something," she said, waggling her phone back and forth.

"Sounds educational. Anyway, towels and sheets are in the hall closet, and anything else you might need, please ask. I want you to be as comfortable as possible while staying here." Savannah maintained a stiff position.

Micki struggled not to smile. She was acting more like a hotel concierge than a host. "I will," she said, straight-faced.

Savannah swallowed. "Again, Chief Blake, I do appreciate the upheaval you've put yourself through to ensure Eliana's—and my—safety."

"*Wow*, you suck at this. I've already told you, it's no problem, *Ms. Castillo.* I want to catch this guy as badly as you do. It's really not that much of an upheaval. Promise."

Savannah huffed, but the corners of her mouth turned up

anyway. "I apologize for *sucking* at this, but I don't frequently have houseguests, as you may have imagined. Especially not under these...circumstances."

"You really don't need to call me Chief Blake. I actually liked it before because it was so formal. I felt like a big deal. But now it just feels weird. I'm sleeping in your guest room." Micki stretched out on the bed, crossing her arms behind her head. Her sneakers were still on.

"Something wrong?" Micki asked, eyeing Savannah. She could tell that Savannah desperately wanted to say something about her shoes. She kicked her feet back and forth so that the toes tapped against each other.

"No, nothing at all. I'll go check on dinner."

"That's great," Micki said. She began moving her feet faster so the tapping leather became louder and louder. "Thank you so much for cooking, it's so nice—"

"My *God*, can you *please* get your shoes off the bed? You've been outside all day! Walking through dirt. Mud. *Vomit*, for all I know. I tried to let it go, I really tried." If Savannah had on pearls, she'd have been clutching them.

"Ha! See, I knew it. Look, Savannah, this isn't going to work if you can't be honest with me. I will definitely annoy you over the next few days. There's no doubt about it. But you just have to tell me. I'm a big girl, you're not going to hurt my feelings if you tell me to knock something off. Clearly, we lead very different lifestyles. You're going to annoy me, too. It is what it is," Micki said, shrugging.

"How will *I* annoy *you*?" Savannah asked. "I may be a lot of things, but annoying isn't one of them."

"Lots of ways. You're annoying me right now, acting all high and mighty about being annoying."

"I am *not* acting high and mighty!"

"Little high. Little mighty. Just saying."

"Listen, *Micki*, you wouldn't know annoying if it slapped

you across the face. You can't see the forest for the trees when you yourself are a majestic redwood!"

Micki scrunched her eyebrows thoughtfully. "So, what you're saying is that you think I'm majestic?" She nodded. "Makes sense." Micki was enjoying a riled-up Savannah, not out of anger but out of comfortable banter. Maybe they'd be able to get through cohabitating with minimal bloodshed after all.

"That's actually not what I said at all. At all."

Eliana crashed through the door, a DVD waving frantically in her hand. "It's part two. Wanna watch it with me?"

Micki smiled at Savannah and ruffled Eliana's hair. "Absolutely. Lead the way."

❖

Savannah looked on as the two of them left for the living room where Eliana insisted upon watching movies on the "big" TV. She didn't know whether to kick Micki out for being obnoxious or laugh at the way she was able to get under her skin. There were very few people who were able to rattle Savannah, and Micki seemed to have perfected it. She left the guest room door ajar and went to her study to tidy up a little work before dinner. And to pour herself a much-needed glass of gin.

She bent down to retrieve a glass from the cabinet below but stopped. The wine stopper lay carelessly next to the decanter. Savannah wasn't sloppy. Ever. She froze, looking around the room cautiously. Nothing else seemed out of place. "Damn it!" she yelled, breathlessly.

A moment later, Micki opened the door. "What's wrong?"

Without looking up, Savannah answered. "He was here again. Look."

Micki went to the bar, searching. "What am I looking for?"

"The top is off my decanter."

Micki nodded slowly. "Okay, is there any possibility that

you left it off? Maybe you got distracted and forgot to put it back on?"

"No, no possibility. I never do that. Never."

"I believe that. I can't imagine he would be so reckless. Unless he wanted you to find it." Micki sighed, rubbing the back of her neck, lost in thought. "Dump it. Let's have a glass of wine. I'm going to check the house real quick."

Savannah swept the gin off of the bar and carried the near-full decanter to the kitchen. As it glugged swiftly down the drain, tears ran along with it. It was so unfair, all of this.

"Hey," Micki called a few minutes later. Savannah was still standing at the sink, the empty bottle next to her on the counter. "There's nobody here. No sign of a break-in. You were only gone for El's soccer game today, right?" She paused. "I don't know how he's doing it." She reached out and gingerly put her hand on Savannah's back.

Savannah turned her head, overwhelmed by sadness and mystification. She saw Micki on the precipice of leaning in to touch her, to wrap her arms around her. But then she didn't. Savannah knew she didn't come off as someone who would appreciate random hugs of comfort, so she couldn't blame her reluctance. But if she were being honest with herself, Savannah would have welcomed it. Micki moved closer and ran her hand up and down Savannah's back lightly before pulling it away altogether. That was protocol when someone was upset, so that was probably the only reason Micki had touched her. Protocol.

"He was in my house again, Micki," Savannah said quietly. "In *my* house, where my daughter lives. This is *not* okay!" Savannah wiped angrily at the unwelcome tears.

"I know. The locksmith is coming tomorrow at eleven. I'll make sure it's something impenetrable, okay? We'll turn this house into Fort Knox if we have to."

"This shouldn't be happening. I don't understand."

"When I find him, Savannah, if I can't catch him, I'll kill

him. No one should be made to feel this way. I'll do everything I can to make sure you and Eliana are safe."

Micki knew saying that she'd kill him was about four hundred shades of wrong, on every level, both personal and professional, but she didn't care. Not at all.

CHAPTER TWELVE

After a fairly quiet dinner where Eliana kept her head down for the better part of it, she and Micki finished the movie while Savannah worked at her oversized desk. When her eyes began to cross at the endless sea of budgetary proposals, Savannah stood in the doorway of the living room, watching Eliana and Micki. Micki was sprawled out on the couch; Eliana was at the other end with her feet pressing into Micki's shins. *Funny*, she thought, as the usual feelings of exclusion and jealousy weren't there. Just a sense of...peace, even amid the chaos. Micki looked up and saw her, gave her a smile. "You heading upstairs?"

"Soon. I was just going to have one more glass of wine, and then I'm done for the night."

"I'll join you," Micki said, giving Eliana a little clap on her calf as she rose from the couch.

The study was warm and rich by design. Savannah loved the deep reds and browns that accented the cherry-stained hardwood floor. She'd had the merlot area rug special-ordered with hand-crafted drapes to match. The study was where Savannah liked to center herself after a long day at the office or after a grudge match with an ingrate. Either way, the room helped to calm her.

Micki thanked her for the wine and took a seat on the love seat; Savannah sat across from her on the wingback and crossed her legs. She let out a sigh and threw her head back against the chair.

"You okay?"

"Just tired. In many ways."

Micki nodded. She cleared her throat. "If this is crossing the line, just tell me—"

"Like I wouldn't?"

Micki tilted her head in acknowledgment and continued. "Where is Eliana's father?"

Savannah uncrossed her legs and sipped her wine. She thought about telling Micki to mind her own damn business but for some inexplicable reason, didn't really want to.

"He's in New York. We had a brief fling while I was working at the *Times* building. He was, still is, as far as I know, an SVP on the business side of the newspaper. Tomás and I hit it off, spent a few nights together, and became a contraceptive failure statistic." Savannah shrugged. "I told him that I was pregnant, and we agreed that I would raise the child alone. I had no interest in a shared parenting partnership with someone I barely knew. Thankfully, neither did he."

"You 'hit it off'? Huh. Does he pay child support?"

"No. I don't want it. Or frankly, need it."

"Did you ever consider not having her?" Micki asked, tucking both legs beneath her.

"No."

Savannah didn't elaborate, and Micki didn't push.

"Does Eliana know about him?"

"Yes. She knows who and where he is. I told her if she ever decides that she would like to contact him to tell me, and I'll arrange it. Thus far, she hasn't had any real interest." Savannah paused. "She's just about the only perfect thing that's ever happened to me without endless planning and design."

Micki nodded. "I hate to ask this, but do you think he could be a suspect? Maybe decided he wants to be a part of your lives after all this time and is going about it in a really creepy way?"

Savannah shook her head emphatically. "He's married. No children. I'm sure he expects a call from me someday. He's been very good about keeping his address and contact information updated through my office. I'm grateful he's kept up his end of the bargain."

"Wow. You don't hear about too many arrangements like that. Is Eliana okay with it all? She doesn't ask a lot of questions?"

"Not anymore. Everything she's asked, I've answered. I don't see any reason to withhold anything from her. It'll just cause her to resent me later on. This is her normal, and as far as I know, she's content. But enough about me. Do you have any family around here? I never see you with anyone but my babysitter and my assistant."

Micki smiled, took a sip of her wine. "My sister lives in Concord. My parents live in Jacksonville. We talk about once a week, sometimes more. They're good people. Dad's a custodian for an elementary school; Mom works part-time in a flower shop. They decided they just couldn't take the cold anymore, so they moved to Florida. We're pretty generic, I guess."

"Generic can be a very good thing."

"I suppose that's true. The less drama, the better."

"Why did you come here?" Savannah curled one leg underneath her thigh. "I mean, Winter Valley isn't exactly a tourist destination."

"I was tired of the city. I never really felt like I gelled with the constant busyness of it all. The noise, the lights, the traffic. It just wasn't me, even though I'd had big dreams of being part of a SWAT team or something when I first joined. I realize that Providence isn't LA or anything, but I wanted to live in small-town USA. So, I saw the ad for a deputy in the paper, which I thought was odd because who advertises in the paper anymore, but decided to check it out anyway. And yay for you, here I am," Micki said, holding her arms out above her head.

Savannah couldn't help but laugh. "Yes. Yay for me. You didn't leave anyone behind? No friends, partners, associates?"

"Well, sure. I had friends, but we still keep in touch. Partners, like romantic partners? No. I dated here and there, but nothing ever really came of it. My last relationship was Stacey, from Country Carpet? She was in sales. Not sure if you know her."

"I don't."

"Well, it didn't end well. She accused me of being standoffish when it came to us. She was probably right. I mean, she was definitely right. But I just didn't feel it with her, you know? Which I know is trite. Not every relationship is lightning and strobe lights, and there's nothing wrong with that. She was great, really sweet, and super thoughtful. I tried but...failed, I guess. I've had relationships, but I guess I just haven't found the one. I don't think I've ever fully given myself to someone. It just hasn't felt right. I think I read somewhere that everyone has three great loves, but that sounds kind of daunting, to be honest."

Savannah nodded. She was surprised that Micki was being so open about her relationship. It was the first time they'd talked about anything so personal. It was actually sort of nice, having someone feel as if they could confide in her.

"But anyway," Micki continued. "That's how I ended up here. Total chance. I just happened to pick up a paper when I was at my brother's house visiting. It was spur of the moment, really. I'm just glad all of that time in the police academy didn't go to waste. Even though working for a private agency pays *way* more money. Hint, hint. At least now I'm like a superhero, basically."

"Can I have a brownie?" Eliana asked, poking her head in through the slightly open door. She held up the bakery package that Micki had bought for dessert.

Savannah looked at her watch and jumped up from her chair. "No! I'm surprised you haven't passed out yet. I didn't realize it was so late. Upstairs, now."

Both Micki and Eliana grumbled at Savannah's direction that it was bedtime. Micki followed up the stairs behind Eliana as if she was lumped in with the parental instruction. They commiserated about the unfairness of bedtimes and late-night snack denials.

"Night, El. Night, Savannah." Micki yawned, closing the door to her bedroom softly. Savannah followed Eliana into her room to tuck her in.

"Are you sure you're okay with this arrangement?" Savannah asked, fluffing her blankets and kissing her on the forehead.

"Yeah, I love having Micki around. She's fun."

"Okay."

Eliana frowned. "What's the matter?"

Savannah stood, hands on her hips. "Nothing. Well, the same thing we were discussing earlier. I'm just concerned about the bad guy that's out there. But I feel a whole lot better having Chief Blake in the house with us," she admitted. There was something freeing about saying it out loud. She did feel better with Micki in the same house. Even though Savannah prided herself on constantly going it alone, there was something to be said for relinquishing a little bit of that solitude.

"Me, too. She does that, you know."

"Does what?"

"Makes people feel better. Like, they don't have to worry anymore, that everything will be okay. Even if it's not right now, she can make it okay." Eliana's heavy eyelids began to close of their own accord.

Savannah sighed heavily. "Yes, I suppose she does. Good night, sweetheart." She squeezed Eliana's hand before pulling her door, leaving it open only a sliver. She straightened her blouse and cast a long glance at the guest room door. For a fleeting moment, Savannah considered knocking and asking Micki to join her for one more drink, even though exhaustion was ready to take over. The thought of lying down in her room alone made her feel vulnerable. She couldn't ask Micki to stay up with her all night, so she decided there was no time like the present. She switched off the hall light as she closed her bedroom door.

CHAPTER THIRTEEN

The sway of the trees. The crunch of the gravel as a car drove down the street. The light patter of raindrops on the balcony outside her bedroom. The creak of the floorboards settling.

All of those things kept Savannah from sleeping. She would start to doze, lightly, and something would startle her. Something as innocent as Eliana shifting positions in her bed. She refused to admit defeat and turn her light on or scroll through her phone. She just lay there, looking up at the shade of the ceiling, gray and crackled in the faint light of the streetlamp.

The lightest knock on her door drove Savannah to a sitting position immediately. Her heart pounded. "Eliana?"

"No, it's me," a voice whispered. Her door cracked open just enough for Micki to fit her head through. Her face looked almost angelic in the haloed light. "Are you okay? I was having trouble sleeping; thought you might be, too."

Savannah relaxed and felt her tightened muscles let go. "Yes, I am. It's much too early to get up, but much too late to take anything to help me sleep."

"Do you want to talk?"

"No, I'm very tired. I just need to turn my brain off for a little while."

Micki nodded. "Same here. Okay, well, good night." She started to close the door again before Savannah stopped her.

"Micki, wait. Would you mind staying in here tonight?" Savannah chewed on her lip. Her mouth had spoken before her mind had processed exactly what she was asking.

"Oh," Micki said, blatantly shocked. "Yeah, um, yeah, definitely. Let me just…let me get the blankets from my bed."

"You don't have to do that," Savannah's heart beat wildly. She threw the comforter down at an angle on the empty side of the bed. There was no going back now; the invitation was out there, hanging in the air like a pregnant thunderhead. She had no idea what the fuck she was doing, but there she was, doing it.

Micki stood completely still, her eyes wide and expression confused. Savannah realized that she had just asked Micki to sleep in her bed. With *her.* That was insane. Irrational. Nonsensical. Strangely enticing.

"Oh," Micki said again. "Yeah, that works. Um, are you sure?"

"If you're uncomfortable with the idea, please don't feel obligated. I'll be fine by myself. It was a silly suggestion," Savannah said, humiliation threatening to swallow her whole.

Before it could get any more awkward, which wasn't possible, Micki opened the door the rest of the way and climbed into the bed next to Savannah. She gently laid her head on the pillow. "Your bed is *really* comfortable," she whispered. "I feel like I'm stretching out on a cloud."

"I know."

Savannah looked down at her flowy silk nightshirt and noticed the base of her neck and the top of her chest were exposed. She wondered if she should change. With Micki in such close proximity, she decided against it. It would probably just call attention to how little she actually had on. She closed her eyes again and felt movement as a leg slowly invaded the space between them, and a knee brushed up against her thigh. Savannah felt the electricity of skin on skin and smirked.

"Sorry," she muttered, pulling her leg back to her own side.

Savannah turned away from her, curling the pillow beneath

her as she lay on her side. It was strange, this, Micki lying in bed next to her. But oddly enough, Savannah felt her eyelids begin to droop, an entirely welcome event.

Micki cleared her throat. "Is this weird?" she whispered, up on one elbow.

"Yes."

A pause. "Do you want me to go?"

"No."

Sensing Micki's discomfort, Savannah sighed. She rolled back onto her other side so she was facing Micki. Micki lay stock-still, eyes straight toward the ceiling, her golden waves framing her face strikingly. Taking a chance, a big chance, a ridiculous chance, Savannah found Micki's hand with her own and tangled their fingers together. She held her breath while she waited for a reaction and was only able to release it once she felt Micki squeeze her hand and take hold, rubbing the base of her thumb gently with the soft pad of her own. Savannah felt a rush of relief, a twinge of gratefulness, and a much-needed sense of security as she finally drifted off to sleep.

CHAPTER FOURTEEN

Once Savannah had finished doling out the necessary phone calls and memos needed for the day, Chloe just stood there in her office, seemingly uncomfortable. Savannah wondered if she wanted to ask if anything else had happened but was afraid Savannah would bite her head off for intruding into her personal business. Again. At that point, Savannah wasn't even upset about it anymore. She came to the grudging conclusion that Chloe really had only been trying to help, and she'd actually succeeded.

"Anything else?" Savannah asked, her eyebrows raised.

"Um, no, not really. How are you?"

"Fine. And you?"

"Fine."

"Wonderful. Please let me know when the funding report is ready." Savannah gave her a tight-lipped smile and resumed working on her computer.

"Have they…sent anything else?"

Savannah dropped her shoulders and squeezed the bridge of her nose, sighing. She knew why Chloe was hesitant to leave, but she wasn't overly excited to share the latest details. "Yes. They've escalated their game. The chief has been monitoring my house. She has it fully under control. Thank you for your concern."

"Any idea who it is?"

"I'm certain if there are any solid leads, the chief will diligently follow them."

"I know I've said this before, but I'm sorry that I broke your confidence."

Savannah sighed again, deeper this time. She was tired of Chloe walking around the office like a scolded child, crunching through a thousand eggshells. "I don't like to admit when I'm wrong, as I'm sure you're aware, but in this case, I will. You were right to involve the police department. You should *not* have done it behind my back, but I have a tendency to be…stubborn. So as long as we're clear that nothing like that will happen again, you and I have a clean slate. I'm sorry that I was so hard on you."

"Thank you. Thank you. I was scared and trying to do the right thing. I won't do anything like that again," Chloe gushed.

Savannah nodded before returning her attention to her monitor. Chloe closed the door behind her only to reappear moments later.

"I did have a message for you, sorry. It's from someone named Cori, who says she's an old friend. She'd like to set up a time for lunch?"

Savannah quickly looked up from her keyboard, amused. "Schedule it."

❖

Micki looked at the bulletin board she'd rigged and shook her head in defeat. She'd wanted so badly to have one of those cool link charts with locations and people tied together by yarn or string. But hers just looked stupid. And didn't really make any sense.

"You do know that computer technology has made those obsolete, right?" Savannah asked, leaning in the doorframe of the conference room that Micki had made her command post.

Micki jumped. "Listen, you can't be here. This is an ongoing investigation, and you're tampering with my thought process. And ruining my *CSI* vibe."

Savannah looked down at the floor and smiled. "Did you get in touch with Cori, by chance?"

"I did. Talked to her for a while this morning. Why?"

"She reached out to my office to set up a lunch date. I assumed something had prompted the contact."

Micki's eyes narrowed. "Are you planning on meeting her?"

There was something about the way Savannah was looking at her that made Micki's stomach flutter. "Yes. I told Chloe to schedule it."

Micki nodded and went back to her bulletin board. "Mmm-hmm," she said. She carefully moved the yellow piece of yarn to the pushpin with Cori's name on it.

"Why did you do that?" Savannah asked.

"Like I said, ongoing investigation. You're on a need-to-know basis, Ms. Castillo." Micki grinned to show she was teasing.

"Will you be home for dinner?" Savannah asked, sounding like a wife checking in.

Micki pounced on it. "Why yes, darling, I will. Should I bring anything home for you or the girl? Perhaps some fresh-cut flowers for you and a fancy new yo-yo for Eliana?"

Savannah made a face but couldn't hide her smirk. "Forget I said anything."

Micki laughed. "Yes, I will. Oh, wait. Rebecca wanted me to eat at home tonight because her dad is in town. Apparently, he likes me. But I'd really rather not, to be honest. Gary treats her like a child. It's kind of weird. What are you making?"

"Salad."

Micki hissed through her teeth. "Yeah, I think I might have to suck it up and eat with Rebecca and Daddy Dearest."

"Chicken pot pie."

"I will see *you* at seven." Micki winked dramatically at Savannah before turning back to her board.

"You really are an idiot."

"So I've been told. Let me know before you go out with Cori, yeah?"

Savannah demurred but didn't say no. She stood tall and straightened her suit jacket before heading back to her office. Neither of them acknowledged the fact that Micki had slept in Savannah's bed the previous night. Somehow, speaking the words aloud would make it real. Micki remembered lying on her back, stealing glances at the back side of Savannah every few seconds. Her body had been warm and confused because she was mildly aroused. She'd always thought Savannah was breathtaking, but other than her infrequent fantasies of sexual one-upmanship, she didn't realize just how attracted to her she was. She had tried to drive the thoughts from her mind and body because that was *not* what staying with her was supposed to be. She was there for comfort. For strength. For camaraderie. Maybe even friendship. By the time Micki had woken up, Savannah was already showered, dressed, and downstairs with Eliana. That made it easy enough for her to slink over to the guest bathroom and pretend like it was any other morning. Maybe the whole under-covers-hand-holding was just a figment of her imagination.

Micki sat down at the oval conference table and plugged her phone into her laptop. She downloaded the recorded phone call and saved it as an MP3. She pressed play and sat back in her chair.

"This is Deputy Chief Mackenzie Blake from the Winter Valley Police Department. Is this Coriander Girard?"

"Yes, how can I help you?"

"I'm going to record this phone call, do you consent?"

"I guess so, that's fine. What is this about?"

Micki fast-forwarded to a later point in the conversation, bypassing all of the standard questions and procedures.

"…about your relationship with Ms. Castillo?"

"What would you like to know?"

"How long were you together?"

"A little over a year. Somewhere around there."

"Can you describe the dynamics of your relationship for me, please?"

"Well, I guess I would say that things were good. We had a lot of fun together. We fought, of course, but we knew how to make up."

"In your own words, how would you say the relationship ended?"

Cori cleared her throat. "I broke it off. It all just felt too… settled. I wanted to keep my options open, I guess. So, I packed up and moved to Boston. It was good for a while, then I was bored there, too. I came back and told her I'd made a huge mistake. Begged her to take me back."

"And what did she say?"

"She said no," Cori said with a light laugh. "So, rather than have to see her every day, I decided to just stay in Boston. That's pretty much it. We still talk once in a while. I'd never hurt her, if that's what you're thinking. She'll always be my one that got away. Have you talked to her assistant yet? That guy gave me the creeps."

"Why did he give you the creeps?"

"He was just always around. Like, even on the weekends. We'd go to the movies and boom, what's-his-face was sitting three rows behind us. And he always acted like it was a coincidence."

"What did Savannah think?"

"She suspected that he was into her, but she figured he was harmless enough. And she always said he was the best assistant she'd ever had. Jamie. That was his name."

She continued her line of questions, and Micki glared at the laptop, listening. She'd have to revisit Jamie Gagnon, but so far, his alibi, albeit a weak one, had checked out.

There had to be something she was missing. Just a tiny reference, an alibi that had a few holes. Someone flying under the radar. A past grievance Savannah had forgotten about. *Something.*

Micki closed the lid of her laptop angrily and shoved it

into her messenger bag. Another day, another file full of leads that went nowhere. It was a good thing that town was so quiet otherwise; Micki had been spending nearly all of her time on the stalker. Poor Jack and Billy were the ones dealing with all the uncontrollable roosters and skateboarding infractions.

Micki had to stop by home to pick up her ancient but still-totally-necessary iPod before going to Savannah's for the night. There wasn't much a little 90s alt-rock couldn't fix.

Rebecca was bringing in her mail from the lobby when Micki walked in. Her face lit up. "You changed your mind? I'm sure Dad will be happy to see you."

Micki shifted uncomfortably. "No, I still have a few things to go over with Savannah before bed tonight. I just wanted to grab my iPod."

"Oh, okay." Rebecca grabbed Micki's sleeve before she reached the staircase. "So, what's going on with you and Savannah? Like, what's *really* going on?"

"What?"

"I know you're working on the case; I get that. But sleeping over? And having dinner together? Eliana was gushing about how much fun it is having you around all the time. Are you staying in her room, too?" Rebecca scoffed, obviously joking.

Micki smiled and started to say something but it was too late. Rebecca could read her like a book.

"*Oh my God*, Micki, you're staying in her room? Are you *sleeping* together?"

"No!" Micki yelled and then shushed herself. She regained her composure, though her cheeks were twelve shades of crimson. "Look, I can't talk about this. There's an open investigation."

"Um, yes you can. I'm *certain* that sleeping with the town hard-ass is not part of *any* confidential investigation."

"Rebecca, I am *not* sleeping with her! I just want to be close by, and if something were to happen, it would probably happen in…there. There's a trellis, you know."

"Mmm-hmm. Okay, so you're not sleeping with her. But you want to."

"I have to go," Micki said, shaking her head, mildly amused and wholly irritated.

❖

"I suppose I should be relieved that nothing happened today," Savannah said, applying lotion liberally to her hands, arms, and shoulders.

Micki stood in the doorway, rapt.

"You didn't find anything worth noting?"

Micki snapped back to reality, quickly shaking away the cobwebs of impure thought. "Nothing yet. But he or *she* made a mistake along the way. I'm pretty sure we're not dealing with a career criminal here. I just need to find it."

Savannah nodded. "I'm sure you will."

Micki paused for a minute, deciding if she should ask or assume or just walk away. "So, good night?"

"Good night."

They locked eyes for a fleeting second before Micki nodded, smiling softly. She was about to close the door when Savannah gave a single nod toward her bed. Micki raised her eyebrows in question, but Savannah didn't answer. She simply slid into her side of the bed, folding down the comforter in the same way that she had the night before. Micki took the hint and suppressed a smile.

"*So* comfy," Micki muttered as she pulled the blanket up around her neck.

"So you've said. Is that the *only* reason you like spending the night in my bed?" Savannah asked with a smile but immediately clamped her mouth shut. "Sorry, I was joking. It was in poor taste."

Micki lay beside her, a thousand and one responses flying

through her mind, none of them appropriate. What was Savannah doing? Was she being snarky, hoping to elicit some playful banter? Was she being serious? Micki had no idea, but her pulse quickened. It was meant as light humor, Micki was sure, but with whatever weird vibe had been hanging in the atmosphere over the last few days, it didn't feel light. She decided it would probably be best if this was the last night they slept in the same bed together. Things were getting very murky, very fast.

"It wasn't in poor taste, Savannah. I mean, it *is* kind of strange. Your bed is the very last place in the entire world that I could have pictured myself in. I would have had an easier time imagining myself riding a whale at Sea World. Naked. With wings."

Savannah chuckled. "It has been an interesting few days, there is no doubt about that. I do want to stress, if you're uncomfortable in any way, I won't be offended if you choose the guest room."

"I know you think I'm an idiot, but I'm not *that* much of an idiot. Come on. I'm sleeping on trillion thread count sheets next to the most beautiful woman…with…in a…room…with…" There was no coherent thought with which to finish that sentence. Micki cringed, waiting to be asked to leave.

Savannah's eyes widened, but she didn't acknowledge Micki's compliment. "I don't think I ever apologized for hitting you the other night when I thought it was you who was coming after me. I lashed out. It was completely out of line, and I'm sorry."

"Apology accepted. I shouldn't have been hanging around like a creeper without letting you know what was going on. My lips were nice and full the next day, so there's that."

Micki started to turn over but propped herself up on her elbow instead. "Where did you learn to hit like that, anyway? Did you get in a lot of schoolyard fights or something?"

Savannah laughed. "Of course not. I was a good girl. No

fights, no suspensions, nothing like that. Besides, my mother would have killed me."

"You don't talk about your family much. How come?" Micki asked, wandering cautiously into uncharted territory. Talking about the past was always a treacherous venture, especially with someone like Savannah.

Looking down, Savannah touched a wrinkle in the sheet. "Not much to say, really. I loved my father very much. He died when I was seventeen. He went to bed one night with a stomachache. He never woke up."

Micki gently touched Savannah's hand. "What happened?"

"An aortic aneurysm. It ruptured sometime during the night, and by the time my mother called an ambulance the next morning, it was too late. They pronounced him DOA. Everything changed after that."

Savannah paused, and Micki sensed that she was contemplating whether or not she should go on. Micki rubbed her index finger along the top of Savannah's hand. She hoped that Savannah would continue. It was the most she'd ever opened up to her, and Micki didn't want her to stop.

"My mother and I grew apart. It's strange, you know, you read all these stories about how a tragedy brings families together and causes people to cherish what they have in their lives. It didn't happen that way for us. At first, my mother was so wrapped up in the details, she didn't have time to grieve. When I'd go to her for comfort, she'd find a task for me to do. I had to survive my father's death completely alone. I realized that even when someone says they love you, they love you on their terms. When the time is right, when the situation is right. A parent's love may not be conditional based on what *you* do, but it is conditional based on what the world around them does." Savannah cleared her throat. "I love my mother. I'd do anything for her. But that kind of best-friend-confidant support system is just a myth. I'm convinced. If it does exist, I've never seen it. And that's why I have to create it so that my daughter can have those things in me. Maybe I can be the one to make that happen."

"I'm sorry, Savannah. I had no idea that your dad was taken so suddenly or that you and your mom were so distanced from each other. Have you talked to her recently at all?" Micki asked quietly. Her heart was shattered. Savannah seemed so buttoned up and together. She concealed her losses with expert precision.

"You mean about this whole thing? I did, actually. Just the other day. She even offered to come here to stay with me. It was so nice to have that option for once."

"But you didn't take her up on it?"

Savannah shook her head. "No. I want to work on our relationship under different circumstances. I don't want to feel like there's a *cause* for her affection. It needs to happen organically, or it won't happen at all."

"It's a good first step, though. I'm sure once she sees the woman you've become and the mother that you are to her granddaughter, she'll realize how much time she's wasted being away from you. Both of you." Micki searched the depth of Savannah's eyes for something other than sadness but found nothing else.

"Maybe. We'll see." Savannah smiled. "We should get some sleep. I have meetings all day tomorrow, and I'm sure you have holograms to consult with."

Micki laughed softly. "We really should invest in some of those cool things they have on TV. Imagine how quickly we would have solved this if I had a psychic on the payroll?"

"Good night, Micki."

"Night."

Micki rolled onto her side, facing the wall. She wanted to turn over, to pull Savannah close to her, to promise her the safety and trust that she'd been lacking. She knew it wasn't her place to do so, even if she could hold Savannah in her arms. Their relationship was built on sniping and frustration. Micki fully realized that she couldn't solely shoulder the blame for that, if at all, but she wished that she'd tried a little harder with Savannah instead of writing her off as a giant bitch so early on.

Even through the exhilaration of being so close to Savannah and that light floral scent infiltrating every aspect of Micki's existence, she felt calm, peaceful. She wouldn't allow herself to think about the state of their relationship once this was all over. What would it feel like to go back to "Chief Blake," who only saw Savannah when she was picking up Eliana or at council meetings where she would attempt to embarrass her in front of the entire town, or the times she would just scoff at her if Micki needed something approved at her level? Bad. She was pretty damn sure it would feel *bad*. Would things go back to the way they were before? Could they?

As her thoughts became restless, she felt movement as Savannah's hand made its way slowly through the space between them where it rested lightly on Micki's hip. Micki sucked in her breath and steeled herself, a mannequin, so there was no chance that her hand would accidentally move away.

CHAPTER FIFTEEN

Morning light filtered into the bedroom. Savannah shifted slightly, coming up slowly from her appreciated state of unconsciousness. When she finally did open her eyes, she looked down to find a feminine hand splayed out on her bare stomach. Her nightshirt must have ridden up at some point during the night, but she didn't feel any urgent need to cover herself. Micki had called her beautiful. It could have been a statement, a thought, something Micki had simply noted. Or maybe she meant something more. Maybe she had meant that she was attracted to Savannah, and that would certainly complicate things. More than they were already. Savannah felt a surge of elation that she didn't want to rationalize. It was easier to ignore it.

She sighed, unwilling to let her thoughts scatter like seeds in the wind. There was no need to dwell; Savannah just wanted to enjoy the comfort of having someone safe in bed with her. Micki was a security blanket; that was all.

Safe. Not a word she would have assigned to Mackenzie Blake three months ago, hell, three *weeks* ago. She was the enemy. An adversary. Someone who would always push back against her, someone who never backed down like so many others did. Someone who would take her down at a moment's notice. It was possible, Savannah realized, that the fear of Micki being some cartoon villain with a nefarious plot against her was all in her head. It was exhausting, assuming the worst all the time. But it was safer. That fear of Micki had suddenly lifted like a bad dream; Micki no longer seemed like a wolf in sheep's clothing. Maybe she really *was* who she presented herself to be. That was a concept Savannah wasn't altogether familiar with.

Micki stirred, her hair still blanketing her face. She twitched her hand and opened one eye just enough to see Savannah lying next to her. Savannah pretended not to notice. When she felt Micki rest her palm against her exposed skin, her first instinct was to pull back, afraid that Micki would think she'd planned it that way. But for reasons she couldn't articulate that early in the morning, she didn't. She closed her eyes again and let the feeling of Micki's thumb moving back and forth, slowly, gently wash over her. Her stomach tumbled, and her pulse quickened. She felt Micki skate her fingers over the cavern of Savannah's belly button; Savannah's breath unconsciously hitched. So, now Micki would know she *was* awake. And letting Micki openly explore her body.

Micki continued her feather-light touches, her index finger tracing a line from Savannah's sternum to the top of her panty line. Savannah's appreciative "Mmm" escaped from her lips before she could rein it in. She pushed and pushed at the thought that kept trying to break through, to ruin the moment. *What does this mean?*

"Mom!" A voice came loudly from down the hall, shuffling footsteps accompanying it.

Micki grunted loudly as Savannah shoved her forcefully out of the bed and onto the floor.

The door burst open, a pajama-clad Eliana standing in the doorway.

"We have no juice."

"I'm sure we do, Eliana; why don't you go back downstairs, and I'll be down in a minute."

Micki groaned, her knees crunching as she pulled herself up to all fours.

"Micki?"

"Hey, El. Sorry about the juice. I finished it last night before bed."

"Um, what are you doing in my mom's room?" Eliana narrowed her eyes first at Micki, then at Savannah.

"Oh, I was just looking for my sunglasses. Couldn't find them in my room." Micki stood, pulling her T-shirt down a little tighter.

"Under Mom's bed?"

"Yep."

"Why would they be there?"

Micki shot a glance at Savannah, who sat with the covers up to her chest. She couldn't hide her amusement at watching Micki trying to outmaneuver a seven-year-old. She didn't feel the need to step in. Micki was on her own.

"During one of my house checks last night, probably."

"But it was night."

Micki threw her hands up in exasperation. "And they're not here, so I guess you're right. It was a stupid place to look."

Eliana nodded slowly, apparently satisfied. "So...can you go get more juice?"

"Sure. I can drop you off at school as long as your mom's okay with that. We can get some on the way."

Eliana watched them both for a second, then turned and walked out of the room, her brow furrowed.

When Eliana's footsteps reached the downstairs landing, Micki turned back to Savannah. "That hurt, you know! You could have just told me to get up."

"There was no time. She was coming, I panicked." Savannah shrugged, smiling sheepishly.

Micki smiled back, trying to straighten her hair with her fingers. "So, when we were lying there..."

Savannah jumped out of bed, fumbling with the clock on her nightstand. "It's *what* time? I have to get in the shower. Please be sure to get something with a low sugar content when you stop for juice." She hastily grabbed a few articles of clothing and closed the bathroom door behind her.

❖

The Early Bird Kitchen was buzzing as usual when the lunchtime rush settled in. Micki sat at a table in the back corner, Chloe across from her. They were trying to devour their wrap specials in record time so Chloe could get back to the office without exceeding her strict forty-five-minute lunch break.

"I know you can't say much, but do you have any idea yet who's doing this to Savannah?" Chloe asked, dragging a French fry through her bloody pond of ketchup.

"Few leads but nothing concrete."

"It's so scary," Chloe said. "I don't know what I'd do if it was me. They've even been in her house?"

"Yeah. Not since I've been staying there, I don't think, but yeah, before that." It wasn't necessarily true. The incident with the gin played on her mind, but she couldn't be certain Savannah hadn't forgotten to put the stopper back in, even though she said she had.

Chloe looked up slowly. "You're staying there? At Savannah's house?"

Micki cringed, feeling as if she'd already said too much. It was like walking a tightrope. She was a little surprised Rebecca hadn't said anything to Chloe yet. "Yes, just for the time being. If I can catch this psycho in the act, it'll be a lot easier for everybody."

"Um, is that procedure? For the police chief to hole up at the victim's house during an investigation?" Chloe raised her eyebrows and took a bite of her sandwich.

"Of course not. But she has a young daughter, and it's a small town, so I have kind of a vested interest."

"Aha. So, if any crime takes place where a child is involved, you'll be moving in with the family. Got it. I have to be honest, though; I know Savannah can be such a raging bitch toward you, I'm surprised she even allowed you into the house. She's a good boss, she really is, but her personal interactions suck out loud."

Micki suddenly felt uncomfortable. Talking about Savannah in that way felt oddly disloyal. "Actually, she hasn't been bitchy with me at all. I mean, the usual digs and snark, but that's just who she is. I think we might have hit a turning point in our relationship. You know, in our association with each other or whatever."

"Well, of course she isn't being bitchy with you. She needs you. It wouldn't do any good to be an ass to someone who is actively trying to help."

"It's not just that, Chloe." Micki pushed her hair behind her ear. "I think that we might be embarking on something like… friendship?"

Chloe winced, a tight smile on her lips. "I love you, Mick, you know I do. You're one of my best friends in the world. And I like Savannah. But has it crossed your mind that she might be using you, for lack of a better word? She can be very manipulative."

Micki felt heat rising in her cheeks. "I don't think so. Not this time. And why are you saying all of this? I thought you told me things were going well? What's your problem?"

"Whoa, what's wrong? Are you offended? I wasn't saying you are naïve or blind; it's *her* I was talking about."

"I know who you were talking about."

Chloe threw down her napkin, their lunch taking an awkward turn. "Okay, well, I'm sorry. I didn't mean to upset you. I have to get back to the office. Lunch is on me," she said, taking a few bills out of her purse.

They said their good-byes, but Micki stayed in the booth, nursing a giant glass of strawberry lemonade. Why *did* she get so upset at the things Chloe was saying? It wasn't a secret; Savannah could be…mean. And manipulative. And cold. Chloe didn't say anything Micki hadn't said a hundred times in the past. Micki closed her eyes and rested her head on her fingertips as she tried to get her emotions in check. Her sleeping arrangements could be clouding her judgment. Being so close to her, touching her body, smelling her skin. Micki wasn't thinking clearly. She had to put a stop to it. That night, whether she wanted to or not, she would sleep in the guest room. Her mood soured just thinking about it. She wanted to just be able to climb in with Savannah, really, *really* wanted to, but after Savannah's abrupt avoidance that morning, and all those foreign feelings that were sweeping over her at the diner with Chloe, Micki had to stick with the decision that it would be best if they slept apart. She found herself craving Savannah's touch, and if she were honest, wanting more, and that could only end in heartache and confusion. She didn't allow herself to process the intent behind it, just chalked it up to hormones and an insanely attractive woman in such close proximity. Micki had always been adept at lying to herself. It was one of her sharpest abilities.

❖

The sound of hammering caught Savannah off guard as she walked up the front steps to her house. She opened the door to find Micki on the other side, a nail in her mouth and tape measure up against the wall.

"Micki, *why* are you hammering nails into my wall?" Savannah asked, incredulous.

"Alarm system," Micki said, her words muffled around the nail sticking between her lips.

"Maybe you could have, I don't know, *asked*?"

Micki finished mounting the bracket, ignoring Savannah for the time being. She tested the sound, pressing a small button on the back of the unit. A high-pitched wail immediately filled the house, leading Savannah to cover her ears. Micki turned it off.

"Well, the sound works. It's a motion detector. We can set it before bed and turn it off when we leave. How come you've never considered having a professional alarm installed?" Micki asked, gathering up her tools.

"Never needed it," Savannah said sadly. "I've never felt anything but safe in this town. Obviously, that has changed dramatically."

"The new locks were installed this morning. Here are the keys." Micki pulled two keys attached to a red carabiner out of her pocket.

"Thank you."

Micki touched her shoulder. "You're welcome. Oh, and I made the alarm code easy to remember. The happiest and most thrilling day of your life."

Savannah raised an eyebrow. "I think Eliana's birthday will be an easy code to crack, no?"

Micki shook her head, grinning widely. "No, it's not Eliana's birthday. It's 1120. The day I officially moved to Winter Valley."

Savannah rolled her eyes back so fervently she thought they might be lodged there permanently. "You are really a piece of work." She couldn't help but smile at Micki's obvious glee.

"So, hey. I feel like we should get out of the house tonight. Just, you know, away from the stress. Do something that Eliana would enjoy, too," Micki added hastily off of Savannah's look. She wasn't suggesting a *date*, for God's sake.

"Like *what?*"

"Don't sound so enthused. Well, I was thinking mini golf?"

"No."

"What do you mean, no? Just like that? No?"

"Yes, just like that. First of all, it's fifty degrees outside. Second, I'd rather scrub my dryer's lint tray with a toothbrush."

"Oh, stop. It's indoor mini golf, and your daughter will love it. We can have ice cream after."

"Even with such a tempting consolation prize, I can still comfortably say no."

Eliana walked in, slinging her backpack on the designated hook in the foyer.

"Hey, El! Want to go mini golfing with me and your mom tonight?"

Savannah glared at her.

"Are you serious? Mom wants to go mini golfing?"

"She totally does! And then we'll have ice cream when we're done."

"Yay! Thanks, Mom!" Eliana ran to Savannah and threw her arms around her waist. "Even on a school night!"

Eliana raced up the stairs to change into something more comfortable. Savannah started to follow her but turned back to Micki.

"I may have to kill you for this."

"That's a risk I'm willing to take. Since your hair didn't catch on fire, and your face didn't melt off, I figured you secretly wanted to go. Once you whack your ball into the mouth of a T. rex, you'll be hooked."

An hour later, Savannah pulled her Infiniti into one of the open spots in front of Goomer's Goofy Golf and wondered what horrific things she had done in her life that made karma decide to reward her with *this*. The gigantic clown on the sign waved back and forth with a club in one hand and a bright blue golf ball in the other.

"I'm pink!" Eliana yelled, selecting a neon pink ball from the rack of endless golf balls.

Micki stood at the register and paid for the three of them. She held the scorecard between her teeth while she tested out a few clubs for length.

"I'll just watch," Savannah said, rubbing her forearms.

"Mom!"

"Nope. Come on, live a little. Pick a ball." Micki motioned at the rack as if she was selling a car.

Savannah tried to shoot daggers at Micki again, but her stupid crooked smile was too endearing to really feign annoyance. Savannah just huffed at her and picked out a shiny black ball.

"Great choice! Matches your soul." Micki smiled at her

while she picked out a bright white one, contradicting Savannah on purpose.

"Matches your mind."

"Let's go!" Eliana yelled, dragging Micki by the hand to the first hole. She overshot the hole but happily chased her ball down the green.

"Do you want to go?" Micki asked.

"I've never wanted anything more." Savannah placed her ball on the small rubber mat and gave the ball a weak smack. It rolled slowly down the green and stopped about two feet from the hole.

Micki took a practice swing, then another, then shifted her position. Eliana and Savannah both yelled at her to hurry up.

"These things take time!" She shot her ball perfectly toward the flagpole. Just a few inches shy.

By the seventeenth hole, Savannah had loosened up and, though she would never admit it, was actually enjoying herself. Eliana was having a great time, and Micki seemed to be having fun, too. Maybe Micki was right; maybe they did need a night like this, where nothing existed but the three of them. No stalkers, no selectmen, no roommates. Just the three of them.

Savannah teed up, aiming for the big gray hippo's tongue. If she could just get it in the center, she could get close to the hole. She putted with precision and stood up to watch the ball's path.

"Mommy! You got a hole in one! You got a hole in one!"

Savannah ran down to the hole where her ball was lolling back and forth in the tin cup. She put her hand over her mouth and jumped up and down. Eliana threw her arms around Savannah's waist and squeezed her tightly. "Micki! Did you see that?"

"I did! That was amazing!" Micki put her hand in the air for a high five, but Savannah ignored it and hugged her instead. "Our only hole in one of the night!"

"I can't believe it! I thought I hated this game, but I'm actually pretty good at it!"

Micki nodded. She looked down at the scorecard and

grimaced. She quickly folded it in half and shoved it into her pocket. "Yeah, you did great!"

Once they were finally on their way back home, Eliana rested her head on the back seat, tired from the day and full from the ice cream sundae she'd just put away. Savannah would *never* normally allow that without an occasion, but she decided to make an exception. Just once.

The taillights in front of them were hazy with the blanket of fog that hung in the air. Savannah cast a glance at Micki, who was scrolling through the pictures she'd taken at Goomer's.

"Thank you."

"For what?"

"For tonight. It's the most fun I've had in a long time."

Micki nodded, watching Savannah stare straight ahead. "Me, too. I'm glad we were able to just enjoy each other. You know, for Eliana's sake."

"Right."

By the time they pulled into the driveway, Eliana was out for the count. Micki carried her in, handing her to Savannah at the top of the stairs. Good thing she was still light.

Savannah poked her head into the guest room after she left Eliana's room, opening the door just a little. She watched as Micki pulled down the comforter on the guest bed, her lip curled. "Micki? Do you want me—oh? Are you sleeping in here tonight?" she asked, swallowing hard. She stared at one of the throw pillows cast haphazardly onto a chair.

"Well. I just thought that maybe we should be careful. Because, you know, boundaries can get crossed, and I just want to—"

"No explanation necessary, really. It doesn't matter to me either way. If you feel your boundaries have been crossed, then it certainly makes sense for you to stay in the guest room." Ice dripped from her words. Savannah hoped Micki couldn't see the hurt that she was certain filled her eyes. She sought to remain stoic.

"No! It's not that, Savannah—"

"Good night," Savannah said, closing the door firmly behind her.

She fought the urge to slam her bedroom door. The mature thing would have been to just tell Micki, but there was a definite pattern between them when it came to feelings. They both sucked at expressing them. For a split second, Savannah berated herself for thinking that Micki would be any different than anyone else. And then she remembered that they weren't in a relationship, and Micki was under no obligation to sleep next to her. It didn't matter. Savannah couldn't rationalize the sting of betrayal away. It might not have been reasonable, but reason didn't seem to be her strong suit lately. Clearly, whether they wanted to or not, they needed to have a conversation. Savannah climbed under her covers, trying to force her eyes closed and her mind to just go blank. The latter refused to cooperate.

CHAPTER SIXTEEN

*P*link. *Plink. Plink.*

Eliana mustn't have turned the faucet handle all the way off when she brushed her teeth earlier that night. Micki smothered herself with a pillow, refusing to get out of bed to go shut it off. If she could just fall asleep…

Plink. Plink. Plink.

Damn it. She threw the pillow off and breathed in deeply. She couldn't stop thinking about Savannah, so obviously rejected but so closed off. Walled up. Again.

She wanted to go to her, but Micki couldn't shake part of her earlier conversation with Chloe. *Was* Savannah just experiencing a form of misplaced gratitude? She wasn't one to lavish praise on people, *ever,* so maybe in some fucked-up, subconscious way, this was her way of thanking Micki for being there? The thought made her shudder.

But no. She noticed the way Savannah had looked at her, the way her body had hitched in anticipation when Micki was running her fingers over her stomach. They didn't touch like friends; even the simplest pat on the shoulder was filled with subtext, and Micki was confident it wasn't one-sided. Savannah certainly wasn't an open book, by any means, but Micki didn't feel it was even a possibility that this *thing* between them was imagined. They were both way too old to be acting like shy teenagers stuck in an endless loop of will-they-or-won't-they. The more Micki thought about it, the angrier she became.

This is stupid, Micki thought, sitting up, listening to the damned *plink* of water dripping into the porcelain. She closed her eyes tightly and craned her neck toward the ceiling. Now or never.

She threw off the blanket and stormed out into the hall. She angrily twisted the handle of the sink to a definitive "off" position before marching to Savannah's door. She raised her fist, ready to pound, ready to have the conversation they needed to have.

And then she froze. She contemplated going back to her bedroom but couldn't will her feet to move. She sighed and rapped lightly on the door with her knuckle. If Savannah was already asleep, then it would be that much easier to—

"What is it?" came the response from the other side of the door. Cold, aloof.

"Can I come in?"

No response.

Micki huffed and opened the door, the room in total darkness. It took Micki a minute to adjust to it before sitting down on the edge of Savannah's bed. Savannah pulled her foot away to ensure there was no contact.

"Why are you angry with me?" Micki asked softly.

"I'm not."

"Don't do this. Please. Just tell me the truth."

"It's very late. There's no reason your insecurities can't wait until morning."

"You know what?" Micki asked, standing up. "Fine. Try to get a good night's sleep, you coward."

Savannah shot up like a bullet. "*What* did you just say to me?"

"I just called you a coward."

"I think you should get out of my house. Now. You need to leave."

"No, actually, I don't. I'll go back to the guest room and lie there, staring at the ceiling for the next five hours until I have to get up. Just because you're emotionally stunted and can't have a conversation with me doesn't mean that I'm just going to run away like a little bitch. I'm here for a reason, and that reason hasn't changed." Micki stood indignantly, her arms crossed in front of her chest.

Savannah was up in a flash, nose to nose with Micki, so close that Micki could taste the mint of Savannah's toothpaste. "Who do you think you are? How *dare* you speak to me like that, in *my* house, no less? You're a child, a *thug*, a ridiculous *caricature*, and you have the audacity to call *me* emotionally stunted? You, Mackenzie Blake, are a joke. Get out of my house."

"No."

"Get the *fuck* out of my house."

"Make me."

Micki stood her ground, allowing Savannah's words to roll off of her like raindrops. There was nothing in her venom that hadn't been spouted off before. Only this time, Micki didn't feel as if she really meant it. She was pissed off, and anger was Savannah's most readily accepted emotion. She needed to push her into expressing whatever else she was feeling, and she'd experienced enough as a police officer to know how to do that.

"*Make* you?"

Micki could see the flash of Savannah's eyes in spite of the darkness.

"Yes, you heard me. Make. Me."

Challenge accepted. Savannah breathed deeply, ready to lash out once again. She got as far as pushing Micki by the shoulders, but Micki's strength outmatched hers. Micki grabbed her wrists and held tightly.

"You'll have to do better than that."

Micki could feel the rage seeping through Savannah's pores. Savannah tried to pull back her wrists, using every ounce of her strength, but again, Micki was stronger. She brought up her knee, but Micki jumped back in time, still clutching Savannah's wrists.

"Let go of me."

"Talk to me. Stop running away from your emotions and talk to me about what's going on between us."

"Fuck you."

"If you can promise not to hit me, I'll let go of you." Micki couldn't help the tingle of fear that Savannah was going to haul off and knock her out once she let go.

"No."

As Micki was trying to figure out her next move, adrenaline must have kicked in. She felt Savannah surge forward, her legs wrapping around Micki's waist. Micki nearly fell backward, letting go of Savannah's wrists and latching on to the underside of her thighs to find her balance. Before letting her regain control, Micki's self-defense mode took over, and she turned quickly so that Savannah's back was up against the door.

"Nice move," Micki whispered against Savannah's mouth, which was just centimeters from her own. Her hands free, Micki knew Savannah had the ability to push herself off, pull Micki's hair, or take any number of actions that would cause Micki to lose her current state of domination. She found it interesting that Savannah chose not to pursue any of them. Her hands stayed on the back of Micki's neck.

"Put me down," Savannah snarled, her breath hot and furious as Micki pinned her to the door.

"Kiss me."

Savannah let out a cruel laugh. "If you honestly think—"

Micki didn't let her finish, bringing their lips together in a flash of heat and ferocity. She felt her stomach somersault as Savannah kissed back after a beat, roughly, with a clash of teeth and a strong bite to her lower lip. Micki kneaded her fingers into Savannah's thighs; Savannah pulled sharply on Micki's hair. Time stood still. The fury and rage that existed just minutes before had transformed into unmasked desire. They only broke when the need for oxygen outweighed the need for each other.

Micki rested her forehead against Savannah's, sharply taking in breath after breath. Savannah did the same. Micki was still unsure of what, exactly, had just happened.

Loosening her grip, Micki allowed Savannah to slide down to the ground, though she didn't move away. Her hands traveled from Savannah's thighs to the small of her back, where they gripped tightly. Savannah's hands were still tangled in Micki's hair.

"Okay, yeah. That was unexpected." Micki breathed out, a strangled laugh accompanying it.

Savannah turned her head to the side where she also huffed out a breathy chuckle. "What the hell was that?"

"A long time coming."

Micki smiled again but let it fade when she searched Savannah's eyes. There was something there, yearning, maybe; fear, definitely. Micki tilted her head slightly to the side, her eyes falling back on Savannah's full lips.

It was Savannah who brought them together again, her hand falling from the back of Micki's hair to the nape of her neck, where she pulled just enough to make her intentions clear. Their lips met again, this time soft and slow. Micki pulled Savannah forward so that their bodies fit snugly together, stomach against stomach, mouth against mouth.

If her focus was able to multitask for even a second away from Savannah's melting mouth against hers, Micki would have laughed at the number of banalities she had been reduced to in the last thirty seconds. She saw fireworks; her stomach quivered with butterflies; her fingertips were electrified; she tasted heaven. But it was true. It was all fucking true.

Savannah gasped lightly as Micki pressed them together even more closely. Micki was pretty sure that every ounce of vitriol that had been coursing through her veins was gone, vanished, replaced with liquid heat. Her mouth was scorching at the touch of Savannah's lips. It wasn't enough.

Savannah dropped her hands to Micki's stomach, tugging gently on the bottom of her tank top. Micki shifted, allowing

Savannah better access without breaking contact. She laid both hands on the sides of Savannah's face, positioning her exactly how she wanted her, dizzy with desire. If she didn't slow it down soon, *any* kind of conversation would be left choking on dust.

Whoop whoop whoop whoop!

They broke apart immediately. "Lock yourself in El's room. Now!" Micki grabbed the fire poker that Savannah had conveniently left behind the door in her room and took off down the hallway as Savannah ran into Eliana's room.

Whoop whoop whoop whoop!

Micki flew down the stairs two at a time, landing hard on the bare soles of her feet. She saw the door cracked open and ran through the downstairs, the fire poker held steadily above her head. She checked inside each room, quickly opening closet doors and looking under furniture. Nothing. She went back upstairs, looking in every room for sign of movement, of anything out of the ordinary. Eliana's door was still locked. She ran outside, down the front stairs, trying to catch a glimpse of someone, *something*, running or driving or even just standing there mocking her. *Anything.*

The night was calm and still around her. A strangled "No," shrouded in anger, erupted from her throat. "Come on, asshole!" she yelled into the darkness. "You want to play? Let's fucking play!" She slammed the fire poker against the tree in Savannah's front yard, the reverberations shaking her body.

A few minutes later, Savannah made her way down the stairs and out the front door.

Micki was walking back toward the house. "I mean, is it a fucking ghost? What the actual *fuck* is going on?" she shouted, turning to Savannah, her face blanketed with red streaks.

"I don't know," Savannah said.

"Mom?" a tearful voice called from inside the foyer. They both ran in to find Eliana standing there, tears streaming down her cheeks. "Mom, Micki, what's happening?"

"It's okay, El, it's okay. Something set off the motion

detector, and the alarm went off." Savannah glanced down to the spreading dark spot on the front of Eliana's mermaid pajama bottoms.

"I'm sorry, I didn't mean it! I'm not a baby; I just got scared, I'm sorry!" Eliana began to cry again.

Micki rushed over to her and knelt down, bringing her in for a hug. "Hey, El, don't be sorry. That kind of stuff happens. It's not a big deal, I promise. I shouldn't have freaked out like that, I'm sorry. I just got scared, too, but we're okay."

Savannah's eyes filled at the sight of her petrified daughter. "Come on, honey, let's go get you cleaned up. Micki's going to make sure everything is safe, okay?" She held out her hand to take Eliana to the bathroom.

"Can I sleep with you tonight?" she asked, running a hand across her sniffling nose.

"Of course. We can *all* sleep in my room tonight, how does that sound?" Savannah asked, looking directly at Micki. Micki could feel hot tears pooled in her own eyes.

Eliana just nodded, making her way back up the stairs. She didn't let go of Savannah's hand.

Micki walked behind them, the fire poker still in her grip. The door had new locks. The windows were locked from the inside. The basement bulkhead was padlocked. The slider had a security bar mounted in the middle of the glass. There was no sign of forced entry. Unless Savannah's stalker was David fucking Copperfield, there had to be an entry point they'd overlooked. Micki sighed deeply and decided she'd go door by door and window by window again once Savannah and Eliana had fallen asleep. Micki put her hand on the small of Savannah's back as she and Eliana snuggled beneath the blankets.

Once she was sure they were both asleep, Micki slid out of the bed, careful not to make any noise. She tiptoed out of the room and closed the door as quietly as possible. She listened for a second to make sure neither one of the stirred. They didn't.

As she began to check each room again, frustration built.

She was better than this. She'd been able to solve cases more involved than this one, so what was she missing? The same twinge of fear that she was too involved with Savannah and Eliana, that she lacked the distance needed for a sharp perspective, reared its ugly head again. She shook off the feeling, trying to focus on the entry points that she must have missed. She squeezed the bridge of her nose, trying to decide what to do. *It's too late to go backward.* Micki looked upstairs to where Savannah and Eliana were sleeping and pressed on with her search.

CHAPTER SEVENTEEN

Micki sat at her desk, her eyes heavy and blurred. Every time she thought about that kiss between her and Savannah, Micki's stomach dropped as if she was riding Space Mountain. Maybe it was a fluke. They were both angry and passionate, and they both crossed that very fine line from time to time. She berated herself for acting like an adolescent yet again, but Savannah seemed to bring that side out of her. Neither of them brought it up. Everything was a big question mark.

Micki yawned. Eliana had tossed and turned all night, making sleep near impossible. David Shaw, Savannah's ex-boyfriend, sat in the waiting area looking at his cell phone. When he had finally returned Micki's call earlier than morning, letting her know that he was back from Jamaica, he'd offered to come into the station instead of Micki paying him a visit at his house.

She called David over from the waiting area and asked him to have a seat.

"Before we begin, Officer, uh, Chief, I'd like some clarification. I'm very uncomfortable with being a suspect in something I have no involvement in. What exactly is going on here? Is Savannah okay?" David shifted in his seat, tapping lightly on his knee.

"Just protocol, David. We have to look closely at anyone that Ms. Castillo had a strong personal connection with. Nine times out of ten, these aren't random acts. A stalker someone has never come across in person is incredibly rare. At this point, we're just looking to rule you out. She is okay, yes. You returned yesterday, correct? Can you tell me where you were last night?" Micki leaned forward, making direct eye contact with him. David Shaw was tall and handsome, his shaggy blond hair making him look more like a surfer than a bank supervisor.

"Well, I went to the Early Bird Kitchen for some pie. And then I went home."

"Were you alone?"

"Yes. I did see Savannah's assistant Chloe on the way."

"What kind of pie did you have?"

"Lemon meringue." David crossed his legs, relaxing his posture.

"What time did you leave the Early Bird?"

"I don't know. Maybe five?"

"And what time did you arrive home?"

"Chief, I didn't look at my watch."

"Approximately." Micki didn't break eye contact with him. "Seven?"

"How did you get home?"

"I walked."

Micki raised her eyebrows. "It's still a little chilly to be walking, no?"

"I wanted some fresh air."

"Okay. Thank you for your time. One last question. I know we touched briefly on this in our previous conversation, but would you say that you left things with Ms. Castillo on a positive note after the dissolution of your relationship?"

David blanched, which Micki noted on her pad. "Positive meaning that I was happy that things ended? No. Positive that there were no ill-harbored feelings between us? Yes, I suppose you could say that."

"Did you have a close relationship with her daughter?"

"Not really. Savannah kept that part of her life at a distance.

She was afraid Eliana would get hurt if things didn't work out. I guess she made the right decision." David shrugged.

Micki felt a wave of privilege that she'd been able to develop a rapport with Eliana that Savannah didn't seem to mind. Not that they were together, but still.

"Have you tried to contact her recently?"

"No. We're not really friends anymore."

"Do you have any ideas about who could be doing this to her? Was there anyone that you felt hung around too much or was too involved in her life?" Micki watched his reaction, which didn't change. He seemed impassive.

"No one really stands out. Maybe her old assistant. He used to worship the ground she walked on. But I think he moved. She had this ex-girlfriend that she kept in touch with. Cori. Have you talked to her?"

"I have, thank you. Is there a reason you think it could be her?"

He shrugged again. "She was kind of infatuated with Savannah, too. It's like she has this hold on people. It's probably because she's so cold and shut off most of the time that when she finally thaws, you feel like it's some great distinction. That you've broken through. You know?" David smiled and shook his head.

"Do you feel that way?"

"I did. But once we split up, that was it. I doubt if she'll ever really settle down with anyone. She's too closed off."

Micki bristled. That was really none of his business. "Thank you for coming in. I appreciate your time. If you could leave me the name of the airline and hotel you stayed at in Jamaica, that would be great. Who were you traveling with?"

David nodded, smiling half-heartedly. He scrawled some information onto the index card Micki had passed him. "My father. Golf down there is amazing this time of year. I hope you find out who's doing this. It's a shame what she's been going through."

Micki perked up. "Has she talked to you about it?"

"No, no, as I said, I haven't spoken to her. But it's a small town. Word gets around. Now, if you'll excuse me, I have to get back to work."

Micki watched as David walked out the door and made another note on her pad. She underlined *David Shaw* a few times before throwing her pencil down on the desk. She didn't like his indifference or his blasé attitude toward the whole thing. He was the second person to mention Jamie as someone who might have a motive to do this to Savannah, but Micki couldn't make him fit. Maybe a trip to Connecticut would clarify a few things.

❖

"So, I was thinking, maybe we should invest in something a little more high-tech," Micki said, swallowing a large bite of beef stew. "This is so good. Pass the rolls?"

Savannah handed her the basket of bread. "What kind of high-tech? Laser beams?"

"No, just like, cameras and stuff. I know a guy." Micki shrugged, turning her attention back to her meal.

"Of course you do. I hate that I have to do this. I feel like a prisoner in my own home."

"I talked to David today. I have to be honest, he doesn't give me the warm and fuzzies. What did you see in that guy?"

"He was nice. He enjoyed bike riding. So do I." Savannah paused. "Did you tell me that Rebecca's father is in town?"

Bike riding didn't seem like a good reason for a relationship, but then, she'd never been in a successful one herself, so what did she know? "Yeah."

"Maybe you should talk to him," Savannah said, cocking her head to the side before taking a roll for herself.

Micki raised an eyebrow. "Why?"

Savannah leaned in to make sure Eliana was still out of

earshot. "It's nothing, but he did express an interest in me a while back. He was forward and arrogant and thought that boasting about his power as an executive would sway me. It didn't, clearly. I called him a sniveling weasel and told him to employ his sexual prowess elsewhere. I will say, the situation didn't do much for the relationship between Rebecca and me. What? Why are you staring at me like that?" Savannah asked.

"Um...*why* didn't you tell me that? When I told you Rebecca's father was in town, you didn't even flinch! That's a bona fide motive, Savannah!" Micki tried not to sound angry, but her emotions took over.

"Micki, this was *years* ago. I'm sure he has visited his daughter in the time since that happened. I didn't even correlate the possibility until today when I saw that his picture was printed in the church bulletin."

"Why was he in the church bulletin? And why were you *reading* the church bulletin?" So many questions.

"He was in the bulletin for making a sizable donation to the new steeple project. And I make it a point to read *everything* that pertains to this town. Shouldn't you?"

Micki ignored the question. "But how could you not have considered him as a suspect? You squashed the ego of a big-time guy who was trying to hit on you. Wouldn't he have been at the top of your maybe list?"

"I wish you wouldn't raise your voice. I'm sorry that Gary Raye wasn't at the forefront of my mind."

Micki drew in a breath. "Okay, well, I'm glad you told me about that. I'll definitely be setting up a time to speak with him. Rebecca is going to be *pissed*."

"Ah, the perks of being police chief."

Micki shot her a look. "Anyway, I'm going to set up an appointment to have more security equipment installed. Maybe we'll catch the sonofabitch on camera."

"One can only hope."

The doorbell rang. Micki and Savannah locked eyes for a moment before they both moved for the door. Savannah looked through the glass and then opened the door.

"Cori? What are you doing here?"

"Your assistant hasn't been able to find any time for you and me to meet for lunch, so I decided I'd just drop by instead. I'm not interrupting anything, am I?" Cori asked, nodding to Micki in the background.

Savannah held the door open, an invitation. "No, of course not. This is Mackenzie Blake, deputy chief of police."

"We've spoken on the phone. Nice to meet you, Mackenzie. I'm sure Savannah causes plenty of trouble in this town to keep you busy."

Micki gave her a half-smile and continued to stand stiffly. Awkward. Jealous. But did she really have a right to feel that way? This was Savannah's ex-girlfriend, and Micki was her... nothing. Since neither one of them had the courage to actually have a discussion, they had a tentative friendship at best.

Cori turned back to Savannah, her eyes glossed over with raw appreciation. "You look beautiful as always, my dear. It's been much too long." She leaned in and kissed Savannah squarely on the lips.

"Yes, it has been a long time." Savannah fiddled with the button on her cuff.

It was the most out of sorts Micki had ever seen her. It was almost amusing to see the usually rigid woman lose her stately air. Almost. There was a vibe between the two of them that Micki wasn't fond of. Cori grabbed Savannah's hand and led her to the study as if they were the best of friends, not ex-partners from a half decade ago. Savannah turned and motioned for Micki to follow them.

"Tell me, what is this nonsense about someone following you?" Cori asked, shaking her grown-out pixie cut away from her face.

Her eyes flashed with something wild, something untamed. Micki could understand Savannah's attraction. She didn't like it, but she could understand it.

"It's actually a lot more than that," Savannah explained, giving Cori the abridged version of events.

Micki watched her closely for any sign of a reaction. There wasn't anything other than normal interest, though.

"Oh my God," Cori said when Savannah finished the story. "That sounds like a horror movie. You never dated any ninjas, did you? I've never heard of anyone being so elusive."

"No, I haven't. I'd say the most elusive partner I've ever been with would probably be you," Savannah said, smiling at her. "But definitely no ninjas."

"I can stick around town for a while if you want," Cori said, her hand resting on Savannah's knee. She was bold, if nothing else. "I've been known to take down a bad guy or two in my lifetime."

"As a journalist?" Micki asked, leaning up against Savannah's bar, her arms crossed over her stomach.

"Yes, actually," Cori answered, although she didn't tear her eyes away from Savannah. "If you look through my portfolio, I've had my share of breakthroughs. Who could be doing this?" she asked. She began to rub Savannah's shoulder with her fingertips.

"Were you in town last night?" Micki asked, confused as to why she was having a sudden attack of…heartburn.

"I was. Is this an interrogation, Chief?" Cori asked, smiling brightly.

"Not at all, just friendly conversation." Micki mirrored her smile.

"I stayed at that disgusting little bed-and-breakfast above the diner. That place has really gone to hell. I can give you my room number if you wish?"

"Yes, actually, that would be great."

Savannah shot a glare at Micki, which Micki ignored. She

handed Cori a piece of paper and pen, raising her eyebrows while waiting for Cori to take them. Cori scrawled something onto the paper and handed it back to Micki.

"I'm going to check on Eliana. Have a good night," she said, leaving them alone in the study. Her tone clearly conveyed that she didn't wish them a good night in the least.

❖

Cori watched her as she trudged up the stairs. "What's *that* about?"

"She's concerned."

"Oh, sweetie, that's not concern."

"What do you mean?" Savannah asked, inching away from Cori on the love seat.

"She's into you."

"Oh, please, she is not. She's a professional. She's just doing her job." Savannah pulled at her sleeve, trying to hide the hint of a smile that threatened to form. Micki wasn't *into* her; what had happened the night before was an explosion of pent-up emotions. It was highly unlikely that Micki would actually consider anything as significant as a relationship with someone like Savannah. Sex, maybe. And she wouldn't consider a relationship with Micki, that was for sure. But was it? Savannah tried to stifle the cocktail of hope and panic materializing within her chest.

"Sure, if her job description includes falling for the victim."

"Cori! She is not *falling* for me. You're making me uncomfortable. And I'm not a victim."

Cori laughed. "Then I apologize. She's very attractive. I'm surprised you're not interested."

"I didn't say I wasn't."

"So, you are?"

"I didn't say that either."

"Okay, well, you can be coy all you want. Obviously, you need someone to look you in the eye and say 'will you go on a date with me' in order to know that they want you. Which is what I did because I wasn't taking any chances. I never should have let you go," Cori said, her voice dripping with nostalgia.

Savannah sighed internally. She didn't have time for what-ifs with someone she hadn't wanted to be with anyway. "The past is the past, Cori. We don't need to dwell on it. How long are you in town for? Maybe we can find a time to get together when I don't have to get up for work in the morning."

"For a few more days. Send me a text tomorrow with some times that work for you," Cori said, taking the hint. She stood up and gave Savannah another once-over. "I miss you."

"You're sweet. I'll talk to you tomorrow, okay?" Savannah led her to the door and handed Cori her jacket.

Once she'd left, Savannah closed and locked the door and cast a glance up the stairs where she could hear Micki speaking softly to Eliana. Cori was fun and impetuous and exciting. Savannah's desire for those things was long gone. She wanted something different. She wanted to be with someone who wanted her for—as corny as it sounded—her. Flaws and all. She was tired of being a conquest. For once, she wanted someone to accept her, even if they didn't always understand her. To challenge her but not try to change her. She couldn't settle for less than that ever again. Savannah was tired of breaking her own heart.

CHAPTER EIGHTEEN

O kay, sweetie, that was three stories; you good now?" Micki asked, tucking Eliana in like a burrito.

"Can I sleep with you and Mom again tonight?"

Micki shook her head softly. "Not tonight, honey. We have to try to keep everything as normal as possible, okay? We can't live like we're scared all the time."

"But I am scared."

"I know," she said, brushing the hair off of Eliana's forehead. "But you're perfectly safe, I promise. You know your mom and I would never let anything happen to you. Try to get some sleep. If you really can't sleep, call us, and one of us will come in, okay?"

Eliana nodded sullenly, but Micki could see the heaviness in her eyes. She'd be out before Micki left the room.

Walking back to the guest room, Micki could hear Savannah and Cori saying their good-byes at the door. She listened for a wet smack or any other unseemly noises. She didn't hear any, but the silence she heard indicated a hug might have been involved. Gross.

As the door shut and she heard Savannah fastening the chain, Micki dropped down onto the bed. They still hadn't talked about the night before. Micki was trying to convince herself that their high emotions had turned into lust, and it would probably never happen again. The gnawing in Micki's stomach told her it was likely something different, but she didn't want to acknowledge that. It was too dangerous. And it left way too much room for disappointment.

"Is she gone?" Micki asked when she heard Savannah in the hallway.

"Yes. She left a few minutes ago. You were less than friendly."

Micki shrugged. "Have to treat all suspects the same."

"Is she really a suspect?" Savannah asked, tightening her lips.

"Yup."

Savannah shook her head, kneading the back of her neck with her fingers. "Are you staying in here tonight, or…"

"Do you want me to?" Micki asked.

"Not particularly."

Micki nodded, trying not to look as relieved as she felt. In the midst of the investigation, throughout the day, she couldn't help but look forward to bedtime. With Savannah. All of her plans of sleeping apart for clarity had sailed out the window like the fuzz of a white dandelion. What she wanted to do trumped what she should do. And she had no intention of trying to uncover what, exactly, that meant.

Once Savannah was done with her nightly routine of lotions and creams, she pulled the covers back and slid in next to Micki. The soft light of her lamp cast unidentifiable shadows all around the room. Micki lay comfortably on the Snuggly Soft Sleep Better Cooling Gel Luxury pillow, her feet crossed at the ankles.

"So, do you get any of the old feelings back when you see her?" Micki asked, berating herself as the words spilled out of her mouth. She didn't need to be such a jealous child about it, yet here she was.

Savannah laughed, setting her earrings down on the nightstand. "No, actually, I don't. Cori is a memory—a wonderful, exhilarating memory—but that's all she is. A memory."

Micki scowled but was grateful for the response. She could have done without hearing how wonderful and exhilarating Cori was, though.

"Are you jealous?" Savannah asked, propping herself up on one elbow.

"No," Micki scoffed. "Come on, be real."

"Mmm-hmm," Savannah responded, smile still firmly in place. "What was it you called me last night? A coward?" She asked the question quietly, her voice oozing with sex. Micki sat up a little, clearing her throat.

"It was just—"

Savannah slid closer, draping one leg across Micki's torso so she straddled her. She took the ends of Micki's hair in her fingers and twirled them, her eyes burning a hole right through the cobalt looking back at her. "I think it's safe to say that I'm not the coward in this scenario."

Oh, what the hell are you doing? Micki closed her eyes and cupped both hands around Savannah's thighs, pulling her snug against her body. A bolt of heat jolted through her, quickening her pulse. "So, you're trying to prove something, then? Your fragile ego needs to demonstrate its authority?" Micki slid her hands around, massaging Savannah's lower back, letting her hands trail lower, lower. Savannah muffled a moan and stared back at her, eyes afire.

"My *fragile ego* needn't demonstrate *anything*, Chief Blake," Savannah whispered, the slightest movement of her hips firing waves of electricity through Micki's veins. "The way you submit is almost laughable. If you think you're in control here, feel free to get up and walk away." Savannah ran the tip of her tongue along the length of Micki's neck.

Micki's muscles were pulsating beneath her touch, and she hissed in her breath, angry at herself for proving Savannah's point. But she felt so. Fucking. Good. There was no point in trying to convince herself that she *could* walk away. She was tempted to pose the same question to Savannah but feared that Savannah's obstinacy might win out, and she really *would* leave the room, arousal be damned. Fuck it.

Micki placed her hands on the sides of Savannah's neck, pulling her closer, feeling her breath mingle with her own. She prolonged the moment for as long as possible before any resistance melted away, and she brought their lips together with such intensity that she felt her head swim. The soft, sweet boldness of Savannah's mouth sent every tangible thing around her into a milky haze; the only things that existed were her lips and tongue. They kissed hungrily, openly, feral. Micki was positive she had never been this turned on in her entire life.

"Come here," she whispered hoarsely, pulling Savannah down on top of her, her legs still wide open against Micki's midsection. They began rolling their hips against one another, the delicious friction eliciting both moans and curses. Micki swiftly slid Savannah's nightshirt up the length of her back, exposing Savannah's breasts against hers, still restrained by the maddening fabric of her tank top.

"Jesus," she breathed, adoration mingled with explosive provocation. Savannah parted her lips, breathing deeply. She reached for Micki's hand and brought it up to her chest, inviting Micki to taste the forbidden. Micki moaned, her fingers exploring and teasing, and oh God, was she wet.

Their mouths met again, furiously tasting each other, licking and biting and dissolving into a wet heat that neither of them could pull away from.

"Mom?" Eliana called out from down the hall.

"No!" Micki moaned, quickly clamping a hand over her mouth. Savannah flopped against her, visibly deflated and still breathing heavily.

"Yes, Eliana?" she choked out, her voice thick and full.

"I need you. I'm scared."

Savannah closed her eyes. Micki threw her head back on the pillow. Fuck. *Fuck.*

"I'll go," Micki said, gingerly scooting off the bed. She was dizzy and shaky. Savannah squeezed her hand as she walked away, falling back onto her pillow. "Don't fall asleep."

Holding on to the wall for support, Micki pushed open Eliana's door. Her body was still tingling. "What's up, El?" she asked, running a hand through her hair.

"I heard a noise," Eliana told her, her eyes wide. She still had the blankets pulled tightly to her chin.

"What kind of noise?"

"A loud one. Outside," she said, motioning to her window.

Micki walked over to the window, leaning her hands on the windowsill. She nodded and looked back over at Eliana. "The neighbors just rolled their trash barrels to the curb. Loud *and* stinky," she said, ruffling Eliana's hair. "Nothing to worry about. And we're right down the hall."

"Are you sleeping in Mom's room again?"

Micki froze, unsure how to answer the question. "I don't think I'll be sleeping in there, Eliana. I was in her room before I came in here. We were talking. About work stuff. Boring. It's way past your bedtime, honey. Get some sleep," she told her, giving her a quick kiss on the forehead.

"Okay, I'll try. But if I can't sleep, I'm calling you back."

"You got it. Night."

As she exited the little girl's bedroom, Micki felt a gut punch that nearly doubled her over. She flattened her palm against the doorframe for support. Why was she acting like Eliana's second mom? She'd always liked the kid, and they had a great rapport when she saw her at Rebecca's or when Eliana would come to the station to say hello after school. But they were pals. This felt more like…parenting. Sure, they'd all bonded since Micki'd been staying over, and things were quickly taking on a strange routine, but something felt different. The fact that Savannah hadn't even blinked when Micki said she would be the one to go comfort Eliana was nothing short of shocking.

Nerves began to creep in as Micki made her way back to

Savannah's bedroom. She was still aroused and desperately wanted to finish what they had started, but the niggling fear that was pushing against her rib cage made her pause. They didn't have to define anything. Two people could certainly just hook up with no strings attached. Happened all the time. Micki crinkled her nose. Somehow, she knew there was no possible way to just "hook up" with Savannah Castillo. It wasn't an option, and the flutter in Micki's stomach told her that she didn't want it to be an option. But that didn't mean Savannah wanted anything more.

"She okay?" Savannah asked, as Micki softly shut the door behind her. Savannah had turned off the light, leaving Micki to feel her way toward the bed.

"Yeah, she's fine. Just heard some noise outside. I checked, everything's fine."

"Good," she heard Savannah murmur from her pillow.

"Should we, maybe, talk about this?"

Micki could almost feel Savannah collapse into the mattress. "Now?"

"Well, I don't know. Yes?"

"What do you want to talk about?"

"What are we doing?" Micki asked, sitting on the foot of the bed.

"I thought that was rather obvious."

"I'm serious."

Savannah sighed. "I know."

"I just don't want you to regret anything."

"Micki, I'm forty years old, for God's sake. I'd like to think I know what I'm doing. I may not always make the wisest decisions, but when it comes to my heart, I generally err on the side of caution."

"So, your heart is involved here?"

Savannah sat up, though Micki couldn't see her in the darkness. "Yours isn't?"

The push and pull, it was always like that. Micki wondered

why neither of them could just take the bull by the horns and be honest without needing confirmation that they wouldn't be made the fool. Their walls were evident. Sad. Strong. She jumped in.

"It is. You scare me."

"You scare me, too." Savannah's voice cracked.

"You make me feel things," Micki said, her voice gravel. "Things I'm pretty sure I've never felt before. I know how that sounds. It's stupid and childish, and you're probably rolling your eyes at me. I get it. But I can't do this and have you think it's meaningless. It's not."

Savannah reached out, pulling Micki toward her. Micki crawled up toward the headboard and slid in next to Savannah. Savannah whispered, "I don't think you're stupid. Or childish. Because if you are, then so am I. I don't give myself easily. I have to guard myself because if I don't, and I let someone in, I'm giving them permission to hurt me. I've never truly given anyone that opening. Not really, anyway. And I wasn't sure that I ever would. Yet here I am." She skated her fingers up Micki's forearm, sending a chill through both of them.

Micki slid toward her, placing a hand on Savannah's side. She was immediately met with warm skin; no silky material stood in her way. "Um," she rasped, swallowing hard.

Savannah inhaled, the breaks in her breath signaling both nervousness and anticipation.

"I want you so *fucking much*," Micki said, her voice a full octave lower than usual. She pressed firmly on Savannah's side, prompting her to turn over.

She did, slowly, tantalizing. "Have me."

Micki's breathing shallowed. The only word she could squeak out, in a whisper, was a surprised "Oh."

Savannah smiled, pulling her down on top of her. Micki found her mouth again, wasting no time before immersing deeply, discovering each other anew. Savannah slipped her hands beneath the hem of Micki's tank top, where she tugged sharply, bringing the shirt over Micki's head. She threw it to the floor. She raked her eyes over Micki's upper body, naked and vulnerable. "You're stunning."

The answer to Micki's unasked question was all the invitation she needed, flattening herself against Savannah, their breasts touching in all the right places. Savannah moaned, scratching manicured fingernails up the length of Micki's back. Micki hissed in response, pleasure mixed with pain.

"I need more," Savannah whispered. She used the sides of her feet to shove Micki's pajama pants down to her ankles, Micki groaning in approval. Savannah pushed at Micki's arm, a silent plea for her to switch their positions, to turn onto her back. Micki understood and slowly broke their contact, her golden waves spilling down the front of her bare chest. Savannah pulled herself up onto her knees, placing her fingers in the hem of Micki's high-cut underwear.

Micki obliged, raising her hips just enough so Savannah could make quick work of them, tossing them into the growing pile of clothing at the side of her bed.

Savannah gripped the tops of Micki's thighs. She bent down slowly, placing a soft kiss at the top of Micki's sex. Micki gripped the headboard, everything inside her a contortion of want, of need. Micki sensed Savannah was torn between teasing her and giving in to her obvious necessity of release, and Micki was relieved when she chose the latter. Micki quickly found religion and grasped Savannah's hair, burying her fingers in that perfect shade of chestnut. Savannah licked and teased, gripping tightly onto Micki's thighs. Micki could feel her muscles begin to tighten and tremble and that was when Savannah began to use her tongue in earnest. She concentrated exactly where she knew Micki needed her, and before long, Micki's entire body stiffened with anticipation.

"Oh God, oh God, oh God," Micki groaned, clutching Savannah's hair one last time before she felt her body give in, give out, give up. The intensity washed over her in waves, ripples of pleasure coursing through her body like unbridled energy. After what seemed like an eternity, Micki felt herself go limp, her body rocking with the aftershocks.

Savannah climbed up the length of her body, her lips glistening, a light smile. Micki had never seen anything so beautiful and was certain she never would again. She pulled Savannah up on top of her, clumsy, Savannah falling onto her in a powerful heap. Micki didn't care. She smiled at the sight in front of her and pulled Savannah by the neck to meet her lips once again.

"I don't even...I can't believe...that was the most..." Micki broke off in an easy laugh, her mind completely unable to produce coherent sentences. She pulled Savannah tightly to her, kissing the top of her head, letting everything flow out of her like a waterfall. It was easy to confuse sex with love. And come on, she wasn't in *love* with someone she'd barely tolerated just weeks ago. She liked Savannah now, yes. Lusted after her, definitely. Love was something totally out there, elusive and ridiculous. But that stupid warmth in Micki's chest signaled something different. Something unfamiliar and frightening.

Before she was lost in the anxiety of analytics, she flipped their positions once again so she was on top of Savannah. She raised her eyebrow seductively, eliciting a smile and an affectionate crinkle of her nose. Micki kissed Savannah's neck, her jawline, her collarbone. She thought she might be happy to spend the entire night focused on those three areas, kissing, sucking, biting, her body reacting forcefully even though she had just experienced a powerful release. Then again, maybe not.

Micki found her way to one flawless breast, engulfing Savannah with her lips and tongue. She let her teeth scrape lightly across the hardened peak and Savannah's muffled cry goaded her. Micki kept her position steady but slid her hand down to Savannah's center, her fingers easily gliding through the wetness and then inside her.

Savannah bucked slightly, lifting her hips to allow Micki

easier access. Encouraged by Savannah's actions, Micki slid a second finger inside, thrusting in a relentless rhythm. Savannah's hands were twisted around the sheets, pulling and knotting as her body writhed. Micki slowed her movement, her thumb running languidly through the velvet to find her sensitive arousal. She began to move in circles, Savannah hardening with every soft swipe.

Micki let go of her breast, pushing herself up to Savannah's mouth again. She moved her thumb just a little bit faster and thrust just a little bit deeper as Savannah moaned into her mouth, elevating Micki to some existential plane she didn't even know existed. Savannah brought her legs up, wrapping them around Micki's waist. Micki let out an audible curse as Savannah's reception to her increased tenfold.

Savannah pulled Micki's head down to hers, smashing their lips together in a fury of heat and tongues, wet lips and loud gasps, and it was perfect. Micki could feel Savannah begin to fall as she clutched Micki's neck with tremendous force. She let go, moaning loudly, Micki's mouth still devouring her as she came with such fervor Micki thought she might black out. When her body finally began to relax, Micki let her down gently, caressing her softly as she lay next to her.

They were both silent for a few moments, basking in the afterglow of perfection that still hung like a blanket in the room.

"So, that just happened," Micki whispered, her voice hoarse and spent.

Savannah chuckled, covering her eyes with one hand. "Yes. Yes, it did."

"And it was magnificent. *You* are magnificent. What made us wait all this time? Think of the lost years we've wasted," Micki said, laughing at the bite she felt on her shoulder.

"We hated each other, remember?"

"Hate is a strong word."

"So is determination."

"Well," Micki said, climbing back on top of her, placing soft kisses along Savannah's neck, relishing the quickening pulse she could feel. "I'm glad we've come to our senses. When did you realize that I wasn't *totally* hideous and that you were kinda into me?" She kept kissing Savannah's neck, shoulder, down her arm.

"I *never* thought you were hideous; I'm not blind. The first day I saw you at town hall, I thought about all of the filthy things I could do to you. And then certain things happened, and I...that feels so good...didn't go that route."

Clearly it wasn't the time to discuss their differences in town politics, though Micki wanted to chastise her for carrying a grudge for so long. Instead, she said, "I can't believe you remember that day. It's like our anniversary."

At that, Savannah chuckled and threw her arms around Micki, pulling her close once again.

CHAPTER NINETEEN

Daylight bounced in orange hues off Micki's eyelids. She refused to acknowledge that the night was over. And then she thrust her eyes open, glancing around the room as if she was in a drunken haze. She grabbed her phone from the nightstand beside her and gasped in horror as she read seven thirty.

"Savannah!" she shout-whispered, nudging her softly at first, then escalating to a vigorous shake.

"Mmm," Savannah whined, shifting her position. "Come back to bed."

"It's seven thirty! Wake up!"

Savannah shot up like a bullet. "What! Where's Eliana?" she asked, forgetting all modesty. The top of her breast poked out above the sheet, unnoticed.

Micki, on the other hand, stared unabashedly, her mouth beginning to salivate. Parts of her were beginning to tingle, and she was dangerously close to jumping back into the bed. She shook her head forcefully to bring herself back to the present. "Did she come in here, see us in bed together, *naked*, and run away screaming?" Micki quickly threw her tank top and pajama pants back on, kicking her underwear beneath the bed.

"Go check on her!" she ordered, fighting with her nightshirt.

"Okay," Micki said, heading for the door. She turned

around, made a beeline back to the bed, and leaned down to kiss Savannah fully on the mouth. Savannah was taken by surprise but smiled as Micki pulled away.

"I could get used to that," she flirted, stretching seductively. "No, stop it, go!"

Micki smiled back at her and rushed out of the room. She poked her head into Eliana's room, but her bed was made, and her blinds were open.

"Oh God," Micki muttered. Shame flooded her. She would be mortified if Savannah's daughter had walked in on them. *Mortified.*

"Hey," Eliana said when Micki walked into the living room. She had a mouthful of Fruity Flecks and a cartoon on the television. She didn't look up when Micki said good morning.

"Does your mom let you eat in front of the TV?" she asked, trying to feel out the situation. Was Eliana avoiding her eyes because she had *seen* things?

"No, never," Eliana answered. She still didn't look up, focusing instead on the frogs on the TV.

"How come you didn't wake one of us up?"

"I went into your room first, but you weren't there. I saw Mom's door was closed, so maybe you fell asleep in there again. Maybe Mom was scared or something." She shrugged.

Relief washed over Micki like a tidal wave. "That was it. I totally fell asleep while we were in the middle of talking. My neck hurts from sleeping at the foot of the bed all night. Yikes." She creaked her head back and forth, rubbing enthusiastically at the muscles of her neck. She wondered if she was maybe laying it on a little thick, but whatever. It seemed as if they were in the clear.

Eliana just nodded and went back to her cereal. Micki heard the shower turn on upstairs and backed up slowly toward the staircase. "I'm gonna go throw some clothes on, and I'll take you to school again this morning, okay?"

"Sure," she responded, still engrossed in her show.

"Good. Right," Micki said to no one and bounded up the stairs to Savannah's room. She shut the bedroom door softly and opened the bathroom door. Savannah's silhouette behind the shower curtain caused Micki's body to stir. She rolled her eyes at her own predictability.

She shed her clothing and pulled back the curtain, stepping in behind Savannah. Savannah gasped but immediately groaned at the feel of Micki's wet skin against her back. Micki let her hands roam over Savannah's sides, up her stomach, and over her chest. She kissed the back of Savannah's neck while her hands explored.

"Oh, Micki," Savannah said. "I want you. I *really* want you." Micki's grip tightened, her fingers kneading in desperation. "But you have to get out," Savannah said sharply, removing Micki's hands from her chest.

"What?" Micki asked, crestfallen. It came out as more of a whine than she meant.

"If I wasn't so turned on, I'd laugh at that. We have about fifteen minutes before Eliana needs to be at school. As quick as I'm sure we'd both be, there isn't enough time to get ready and get her there on time. Now get out." She put her hand on her hip and cocked her eyebrow. Micki was astonished at how Savannah could maintain an air of authority while naked and dripping wet. She grumbled about everything being totally unfair before she grabbed a towel from the sink and began to dry off.

With three minutes to spare, Micki walked out with Eliana toward the cruiser. "Mom never lets me ride in front," Eliana said. She shoved her backpack down on the floor and buckled her seat belt with a smile.

Micki smiled back and patted Eliana's knee. "If my back seat wasn't walled in with Plexiglas, I'd stick you back there, too. Your friends are going to think you spent the night in jail, huh?" Micki winked at her and fired up the engine.

Eliana rolled her eyes but giggled anyway. "You're such a dork."

As Micki was pulling out of the driveway, a large white van pulled in beside her.

"SafetyVision," the large man grunted at her open window. His face was mostly covered by the visor, which he had down against his window. "Here to install some cameras?"

"Great. Ms. Castillo is inside; she can direct you. Oh, make sure you ring the doorbell." Micki lifted her hand in a half wave and flipped on the radio, grateful for some happiness among the chaos.

❖

Micki leaned against her car with her aviators on and watched Eliana walk into school. She wanted Eliana to have the full effect of being dropped off at school by the chief of police. The ripped jeans and UNH sweatshirt probably detracted from her authority a little, but hey, beggars can't be choosers.

That flurry of emotion invaded her again. She saw Eliana shoot her a quick wave before disappearing within the walls of the school. It was all very domestic, bringing her to school, having dinner with them, *sleeping* with Savannah. If it wasn't happening to her, she wouldn't have believed it. The most frightening part about it was how comfortable Micki felt.

She got back in her car and decided to head over to the Early Bird for a coffee and Danish. The jellied raspberry was calling her name. She was about to pull into a parking spot when a thought occurred to her, and panic flooded her system.

"Oh my God," she said aloud, peeling out onto Main St. "What the *fuck* was I thinking?"

The van. The nondescript white van with no back windows and a rusted bumper. It could be anyone; it could be *him*; it could be someone hiding in the back with a ski mask and a crowbar.

She tried to remember his face. Nothing. She only saw the

lower half, his mouth and jaw, and there was nothing memorable about either. Micki's heart was pounding. How could she have been so *stupid*?

She flew down Kensington Road, her stomach in knots, and her throat nearly closed. She parked behind the van, thankful it was still sitting in the driveway, and pulled her gun from the glove compartment. She ran to the front door, leaving her driver side door wide open behind her.

The door was cracked open. There wasn't a sound coming from inside the house, so she drew her gun carefully and used her foot to nudge the door the rest of the way.

Silently, she moved through the foyer and into the kitchen. Nothing. She turned the corner toward the back door, a grunt finally breaking the silence. The man from the van was pulling out some sort of weapon from his plain black duffel bag.

"Drop it!" Micki yelled, her hand steady as she pointed her gun in his direction.

The man visibly jumped, letting his drill drop to the ground with a resounding crash. "Christ, lady, I have a work order!" he yelled at her. He placed both hands high above his head in submission.

"Savannah!" Micki yelled, not adjusting her aim.

"Micki?" Savannah asked, as she walked into the house from her backyard through the porch door. "What's going on?"

"This crazy bitch is going to shoot me!" the technician shouted, his voice cracking with fear.

Micki lowered her weapon slowly, looking from the man to Savannah. She looked toward the wall near the back door where the mount was halfway installed above the doorframe.

"Micki, this is Paul. He's here to install the cameras?" Savannah stood between them, keeping her eyes trained on Micki.

Paul kicked a box toward her, the words "SafetyVision" scrawled on the side in bright blue.

Micki breathed out, relieved and embarrassed. "I'm sorry.

I should have checked your credentials this morning when I left the house," she told him as she re-holstered her gun.

Paul just stood there, his hands still raised above his head.

"I'm sorry, really. Please continue. It was a mistake. Sorry."

He lowered his hands finally, leaning slowly toward the ground. "If I pick up my drill, are you going to shoot me in the nuts?"

Micki shook her head, still embarrassed. "No, Paul. Your nuts are safe."

He grumbled and griped something about foolish women going off the deep end, but Micki thought it might be best to just let it go. She didn't really need to deal with a lawsuit on top of everything else.

Savannah watched Micki with faint amusement, her cheeks flushed, and the wild in her eyes slowly taming. "You could have called?"

Shaking her head, Micki grabbed Savannah by the wrist and dragged her into the kitchen. "Yes, because if someone is being murdered, it always makes sense to call them."

"Didn't you hire this company to install the camera? I thought you knew a guy."

"I *did*, and I *do*, but we still don't know who's doing this. It could have been a front, or maybe the real stalker was in the back of the van with a rifle pointed at the driver's head. Too many variables. I should never have left this morning without checking him out. I'm sorry," Micki said. She looked down at the ground, upset.

"Micki," Savannah's tone was uncharacteristically gentle, "you did nothing wrong. We have to live our lives. There's actually something very sweet about your overreaction, but you can't watch over me every second of the day." She reached out and cupped the side of Micki's face.

Micki leaned into it, closed her eyes. "Yes, I can," she said petulantly.

"No, you can't. Like you said, maybe the cameras will catch him. And then all of this can just go away."

Micki brought her own hand up and placed it on top of Savannah's. She pulled them both away and kissed Savannah's fingertips. "I couldn't take it if anything happened to you. I think I'd die."

Savannah gave her a half-smile. "You wouldn't die. Don't be so dramatic. If this had happened two months ago, it would have been like any other case to you. I realize that my sexual expertise has left you dazed, understandably, but you don't have to worry. I've taken care of myself for a very long time. That hasn't changed."

Micki scoffed but pulled Savannah into her tightly. "Shut up, Savannah. It wouldn't have been 'any other case.' I already told you, I never *actually* hated you. And I always thought you were smokin' hot."

Savannah laughed, rubbing her hand softly up and down Micki's back. Their embrace was unfamiliar but entirely welcome. "So, does this mean we're *dating*, Chief Blake?"

"I think it might, Ms. Castillo. I don't make a habit of doing what we did last night with *friends*." Micki chuckled into Savannah's shoulder then let insecurity weasel its way in. She pulled back so their faces were just inches apart. "Is that okay?"

Savannah tucked a piece of Micki's hair behind her ear. "I warn you, I'm not very good at this. I'm selfish and rigid and stubborn beyond reason. I can be relentless when it comes to being right. I'm set in my ways, and I don't share well."

Micki feigned shock. "Well, that changes everything, then. I've always looked at you as the second coming of Mother Teresa."

"Funny," Savannah deadpanned. "But I'm serious. It's one thing to put up with those things in a *friend* or even someone you share a bed with. It's a very different thing to deal with that kind of person in a romantic relationship."

Micki smirked, leaned in and placed feather-light kisses on Savannah's neck. "I think"—*kiss*—"I'm up"—*kiss*—"for the challenge"—*kiss.*

Savannah hummed in approval, tightening her grip on Micki's arm. She used her index finger to raise Micki's chin so they looked into each other's eyes. "I hope you know what you're getting yourself into," she whispered before bringing their lips together in a cloud of heat. They kissed deeply before Micki smiled into it, moving her head back only slightly.

"Being with me isn't always a day at the beach, you know," she said, her lips moving against Savannah's as she spoke.

Rather than respond, Savannah gripped the back of Micki's neck, pulling her more firmly against her. Their bodies melded into one another, their kiss blocking out everything around them.

At the sound of an electric drill, they both startled and jumped away from each other. "God, this is weird," Micki laughed, reaching for Savannah's hand.

"Yes. Yes, it is. Now go to work."

Micki left through the front door, giving Paul another quick nod of apology. He ignored her. She sat in her cruiser for a minute, seeing Savannah's shadow move from room to room. Her heart filled. But what if she'd been right, and the guy in the white van had been the one coming after Savannah? What she was doing was terribly unprofessional and, if she was being honest, dangerous. She needed to focus on her training, on keeping Savannah and Eliana safe. Instead, she was floating through a cloud of excitement and wonder. For a fleeting moment, she wondered if she should put the brakes on whatever this was with Savannah. And then she smiled at how utterly ridiculous that was. She was self-aware enough to know that wasn't going to happen. But enough was enough. It was time to throw herself into the case and take the offender down.

CHAPTER TWENTY

Everything was different than when Micki had been with Stacey, and that scared the shit out her. This thing with Savannah was new, and intimacy had the tendency to seem a lot more intense early on than it did six months down the road. Micki knew that. But even when she'd first started dating Stacey, she never felt as if she was in such a spiral. It was sweet and exciting, but this time, Micki felt different. Though she wasn't as blatant about it as Savannah, Micki liked to be in control. Not over inane things, like whether or not employees could wear white-soled shoes, but when it came to her emotions, Micki was a textbook control freak. Maybe it was just because Savannah was…Savannah. That Micki had been able to break through her armor, even just a little bit, made her swell with affection. Ugh. She felt as if she belonged in a Saturday night movie of the week. *Will she be able to break through the walls of love? Tune in to find out.* Stupid.

Micki picked up the phone while unbending a paper clip. "Winter Valley PD, Deputy Chief speaking."

"It's me."

"Hey, Beck. What's up?"

"Why is my dad on his way down to see you?" Rebecca asked.

Micki could sense the bite in her question. "Um, well, I can't really talk about it. At least not yet. I just need to ask him a couple of questions. Total run-of-the-mill stuff," Micki said.

"You couldn't have given me a heads-up?"

"Not really. You know how these things work."

"Wow."

"Rebecca, I—"

But a dial tone was all that was left of the phone call. Micki hung up the receiver and rubbed her face with her palms. One of the drawbacks of such a small town, she supposed. They were all just scurrying up different strands of the same web.

Micki looked up as Gary Raye walked into the police station, his superiority complex on full display. He frowned at Micki before taking a seat across from her. He stared at her desk with disdain. Any goodwill Micki had built up with him in the past appeared to be long gone.

"I assume you have a matter of great importance to discuss with me, else I'll be forced to lodge a complaint for having my time so egregiously wasted," he said, flicking a small blob of dust to the floor. His three-piece suit was clearly expensive, and he acted as though sitting in the scratched folding chair would taint him with paucity. He was handsome, with gray hair at his temples and a chiseled jaw. He was in his mid-fifties at most.

"Absolutely, Gary, sorry, Mr. Raye. I'll get right to the point. Can you detail your relationship with Savannah Castillo for me, please?"

Raye's eyebrows raised. "Relationship? We haven't one."

"Then please go over any interaction you've had with her."

"As a man of significance in this town, even though I no longer live here, we have had business dealings. Surely you didn't bring me here to debate permits and contracts."

"No, no, I didn't. Were you upset with her when she rejected your advances? Did you feel that your masculinity had been bruised?" Micki cringed as soon as the words were out. For the second time in her interviews, she'd let her defensiveness rear its ugly head. There really was something to be said for being too close to a case. Badgering wasn't a common technique when trying to set a person of interest at ease. Even someone as cartoonish as Gary Raye.

His expression distorted into one of contempt. "I don't know who you think you are, *Chief*, but I'm not someone to be toyed with. Tell me, is this some sort of role-play assignment for your junior college project?"

Micki sat back in her chair, ignoring him. "I apologize, Mr. Raye. I didn't mean to offend you. But I do need to know about the contact between you and Ms. Castillo."

"Well, if you must know, I *had* taken a slight interest in her some time ago. I thought it might give her a little thrill, notching a Raye on her bedpost. She's an attractive woman, certainly, but remember, I have many business partners out in LA. Those women make the women of Winter Valley look like farm pageant castoffs."

Micki swallowed every bit of abhorrence she felt. How this arrogant asshole raised her sweet, trustworthy, humble friend Rebecca was a complete mystery. Her behavior today notwithstanding.

He continued. "I fully believe she rejected me as a way to preserve her own pride. She knew I would never consider anything as trivial as feelings, so she cut me off at the pass. Brilliant maneuver, if you ask me."

Micki'd had enough with the show he was putting on. "Where were you the night before last?"

"At my daughter's house. In your apartment, which you would have known, had you not been brownnosing Ms. Castillo. I've seen people do many things to advance their careers, but I must say moving in with someone is a first."

"I didn't move..." Micki trailed off. "You know what? Thank you for your time. Please see yourself out."

She scribbled *confirm with Rebecca* on her notepad before storming outside to get a breath of fresh air.

Micki watched as Raye pulled out of the police station in

his Lexus, speeding off toward the highway. She sincerely hoped that the interest in her father wouldn't drive a wedge between her and Rebecca. She was the first friend Micki made when she moved to Winter Valley. They'd met at the mailboxes when Micki was still living in the basement studio she'd rented. It was the only apartment available without a twelve-month lease, and at the time, she wasn't sure she should commit to anything. What if Winter Valley ended up being like Twin Peaks? Although lately, that notion was hitting a little closer to home than Micki cared to admit. She decided she'd catch up with Rebecca later that night. There was no reason for them to be at odds just because her father turned out to be a lecherous dick.

The gifts Savannah had been receiving were tainted with emotion, and Gary Raye was pretty emotionless. Micki didn't see him as a viable suspect, but her list was pretty short as it was. There was an ex-boyfriend who'd been in Jamaica, an ex-girlfriend who'd been in town but didn't seem to have any kind of motive, and an ex-assistant who lived two hours away. Micki sighed heavily before trudging back to her desk.

"Chief," Billy called, waving a folder in the air. "Here are those hotel records you requested."

Micki took the file back to her desk and read through the Jamaican resort's records. David Shaw had checked in and out on the days he'd said he had. Micki snapped the folder shut and shoved it into her desk drawer. What the hell was she missing?

CHAPTER TWENTY-ONE

The scent of Moroccan oil–infused shampoo tickled her nose. Savannah opened her eyes sometime before dawn, taking a moment to familiarize herself with her surroundings. She was in her bed, as usual, but the sensation of tangled limbs around her own was still alien. Micki was lying on her stomach facing the other way, but her arm was wrapped tightly around Savannah's waist, and their lower halves were pretzeled. Savannah ran her fingers lightly along Micki's arm, feeling more comfortable in her embrace than she could remember. Maybe ever. Probably ever.

That a catastrophe had delivered this woman to her in such a way was almost fitting. That's what they'd always been to each other—absolute disasters. The fighting, the one-upping, the demeaning. The thinly veiled sexual tension that always ended with insults and dirty looks. All of that seemed like a lifetime ago. She'd been more open with Micki than she'd been with anyone in a long time. Her relationship with David was real, but scattered on the surface. With Cori, the love was there, but there was never a promise of tomorrow, and that had worked for them. Before that, she'd had a series of near misses, a few maybes, no definites. That was all. And then Micki had come along, and Savannah was questioning everything she thought she knew.

Micki stirred gently, so Savannah lifted her fingers not to wake her. Micki muttered something in her sleep, and instead of letting her go, tightened her hold. She couldn't make sense of this. Her feelings were unexpected and growing exponentially but were shrouded in uncertainty and fear. It was all happening too fast. Savannah had never in her life jumped into a relationship before. That kind of life event took careful planning and consideration. When all of this went away, *if* all of this went away, would Micki go with it? Eliana was clearly attached to her, but she had been before all of this had started. Savannah honestly believed Micki wasn't the type to just pretend that Eliana didn't exist, even if things between them fizzled, so Savannah was comfortable that Eliana's feelings were protected. Still, control was such an integral part of Savannah's being, and all of these external forces were pinning her to a wall. Without Micki to ground her, Savannah wondered if she would have spun out completely with the stalker invading the areas of her life she'd worked so hard to keep private. Not that she was in control of her feelings around Micki, either. She wanted to trust her, to let her in, but she didn't know if she'd survive the aftermath of being let down, of that inevitable heartbreak one more time. But this time Savannah didn't know how to stop it. She didn't want to just walk away or rebuild the walls Micki was carefully dismantling brick by brick. She wanted to believe what she was feeling, as terrifying as it was.

As Micki shifted again, her foot lodged comfortably behind Savannah's knee, Savannah smiled and slid her arm beneath Micki's. For now, the only thing to do was to allow it. To feel it. Warm. Protected. Loved. She'd deal with the emotional fallout later.

❖

Cuppa Joe's was bustling as usual. Micki saw David Shaw sitting at one of the outdoor patio tables sipping on an iced coffee and eating a scone. He looked up, and their eyes locked, so just ignoring him was off the table.

"Hi, David," she said, nodding once at him. "How are you?"

"Fine, thanks. Enjoying the sunshine," he said. He shaded his eyes with his hand and looked up at the sky. "Feels like spring."

"It does. Well, have a good one," Micki said. She pushed through the door and spotted Savannah sitting at a table by the fireplace. Her stomach did a flip-flop at the sight of her in her black suit with a white collared shirt poking out, scanning a newspaper with her reading glasses perched low on her nose.

"Hi." Savannah smiled, folding up the paper. "I ordered you a coffee and a cheddar bagel."

"Interesting choice," Micki said. She smiled, remembering their last encounter over a cheddar bagel. How times had changed.

"Did you see David out there?" Savannah asked.

"Yeah. Did he talk to you?"

"He looked surprised to see me. Asked how I'd been. Told me he'd heard about my recent troubles and offered to help if he could." Savannah shrugged and took a long sip of her cappuccino.

"That was nice of him, I guess. Did it seem weird to you?"

"He seemed sincere enough. This whole thing is weird. No one who knows what's going on knows how to act around me."

"You look really good today. Just saying." Micki winked at her and bit into her bagel.

Savannah laughed. "Thank you. So do you, actually," she said.

Micki had on her regular baby blue, short-sleeved uniform shirt with her navy dress pants. She had spent a few extra minutes on her hair, though. Savannah reached across the table and tugged on a strand of Micki's waves. Micki quickly scanned the restaurant to see if anyone had been watching.

"What? Are we having a clandestine affair that I'm supposed to keep secret?"

Micki snorted. "No, but I don't want anyone to think I'm taking advantage of you. Especially since I'm the lead investigator—yes, I know, *only*, you don't have to say it—on your case. It might appear unseemly."

"Unseemly?" Savannah kicked off one of her heels and ran her foot up the length of Micki's leg, walking her toes up toward the top of Micki's thigh.

Micki almost choked on her bagel. "Savannah!"

A few heads turned. Savannah brought her leg back down and raised her eyebrows at Micki. "If you want to make sure no one thinks you're taking advantage of me, I can put that fear right to rest. Don't test me."

And just like that, Micki was completely turned on again. Savannah possessed the ability to arouse her as if she carried around a flashing sign with an arrow that read, "Switch located here."

"Fancy meeting you here," a voice called from behind Micki.

Savannah looked up in surprise. "Cori! What are you doing here?"

"I'm only in town for a few more days, so I've been trying to hit all of the old haunts. Chief, you still haven't come by my hotel room for that little visit you mentioned. Clock's ticking," Cori said, clicking her tongue. She had on skinny jeans and an off-the-shoulder sweatshirt. She winked at Savannah and made the "call me" sign with her index and pinky fingers. Micki hated her a little bit more every time she saw her.

"God, it's like old home day in here. The lost loves of Savannah Castillo. What did you ever see in her?" Micki asked. She tried to keep the look of disgust at bay but knew she'd failed.

"She was what I needed at the time. She was fun and easy, and I didn't have to put on airs around her. It was a nice defection from my usual routine. Why haven't you gone to her hotel room?"

"To be perfectly honest, I don't really have a reason to. I was, maybe, posturing a little that night in your study. She answered all of my questions, so I don't really have anything else that won't make it seem like I'm harassing her. But I have faith in myself; I'm sure I'll come up with something."

"Mature."

"No shame in my game."

"I have to get to the office," Savannah said, lifting her laptop bag from the windowsill beside her. "I'll call you later."

"'Kay. I'll miss you."

"Shut up."

Micki turned to watch Savannah swagger out of the coffee shop, unable to wipe the smile from her face. As she left the diner, she was glad she wouldn't have to make small talk with David since the seat where he had been drinking his coffee was now empty.

CHAPTER TWENTY-TWO

Chloe poked her head into Savannah's office, invited in by a simple nod. She handed Savannah a manila envelope, once again with no postmark or proper addressing. Savannah looked up when she saw the package.

"Where did this come from?" she asked, her heart beginning to beat faster.

"I found it in the lobby. I was just going to ignore it, but I thought that it might contain something that Micki could use to find them. It's been a while since we've had anything show up here." Chloe fidgeted nervously.

"Yes, it has been a while," Savannah muttered, looking the package over. "They seem to have taken a liking to coming directly to my house instead."

"I'll leave you alone."

"You don't have to go. I should probably have a witness, in case I inadvertently inhale anthrax or something similarly fatal," Savannah said. She tried to smile but was unsuccessful.

Chloe nodded, sensing her anxiety. She took a seat at Savannah's desk, watching with anticipation.

Savannah slid her fingernail underneath the seal, sighing before she poured the contents out onto her desk. An ornate gold mirror spilled out onto her desk, the familiar cherubs holding up a smiling sun on either side. A message, written in red lipstick, was scrawled messily on the otherwise pristine surface.

don't take my sunshine away

She gasped, recognition firing to the surface.

Chloe raised her eyebrows. "What is it? It looks like the mirror in the office. Do you know what it means?"

Savannah pushed the mirror off to the side and reached for her cell phone. She met Chloe's eyes and said simply, "Jamie."

That sonofabitch. Savannah fought the urge to smash the mirror which seemed to be mocking her from her desk.

"The assistant that I replaced?" Chloe asked.

Savannah nodded. "I'm going to call Micki to tell her about this. Shut my door on your way out, please?"

Chloe paused but left the office. Savannah stood, grimacing at the offensive object. She wanted to go tear down its larger mate hanging in the lobby but decided she should probably wait until he was caught before doing anything so drastic. She was angry with herself because even though she knew Jamie was a weasel, she couldn't wrap her head around him doing anything so depraved. She rolled her neck, releasing the fists she'd been making unconsciously at her sides. She had a phone call to make.

❖

Scrolling through the app store on her phone, Micki finally found the SafetyVision app that she needed. She logged in with her credentials and waited for the images to appear on her phone.

It seemed that even though she had scared Paul half to death, he'd done an okay job installing the cameras. She could see Savannah's backyard, though the images were grainier than she would have liked. She'd need to contact them about that. For the price of those things, the images should have been in 3D. Everything was still and serene.

Micki pulled out the pamphlets she'd brought in from

Savannah's house, detailing all of the things the app could do. She rewound the time to eight p.m. the previous evening, but everything still looked the same. Just darker.

She yawned as she slowly dragged her pointer finger along the bottom of her screen, the minutes ticking by. An adorable little raccoon waddled through the yard into the woods behind her house. A couple of leaves skirted by, floating like feathers. And then at two a.m., there he was.

Micki's mouth dropped open, and she gasped in surprise. He stood there, looking into the camera, brazen and unflinching. Micki could now comfortably rule out Cori as a suspect. She couldn't make out much with the Stalker 101 outfit of dark pants and a bulky black hoodie, but the broad shoulders, wide stance, and straight frame were clearly male.

The face was covered almost completely by the hood drawn forward, and shadows created gray splotches where any distinguishing features might be. This person knew he was being filmed or, at the very least, appearing on a live camera. And he just stood there, unmoving. Daring someone to confront him. Micki felt a light sweat prickle on her forehead. Her office phone lit up alongside its shrill ring, and she quite literally jumped out of her seat.

"Hello?" Micki answered, clearing her throat. "Blake speaking."

"It's me. Something else came, and it's from Jamie."

"Whoa, slow down. How do you know?" Micki asked, pausing the screen on the man in the hoodie.

"It's a replica of a gift he gave me when he was working for me. If that doesn't send a message, I don't know what does. I guess he grew tired of hiding in the shadows."

"Okay. Bring it over. I have the guy on tape, too." Micki pulled up Jamie's Facebook profile and scrolled through his pictures. It could have been him, but she couldn't conclude anything from the photos.

"What? Oh my God. Okay, I'm coming."

Micki stood and made another call, the ancient beige phone cord wrapped around her waist as she paced. She saw Savannah walk through the door and motioned her over. "Middletown Police Department," she mouthed to Savannah. "Thanks, Sargent. Yes. Of course. Any information would be greatly appreciated. Sure, I'm available on my cell at any time. Thanks again."

Savannah listened as Micki hung up the phone and wrote furiously on her notepad, untangling herself from the cord before the receiver crashed to the ground.

"They're going over to his house now," she told Savannah without looking up from her notes. "If he's home, they'll find him. The Middletown PD is actually very helpful."

"Good," Savannah said. She sat uncomfortably in a hard wooden chair. "I don't understand why he would do this. It's been a long time. But at least we know."

Micki leafed through her notebook, shaking her head. "His alibi wasn't airtight by any means, but based on my intel, he's only been here sporadically over the last few weeks. Presumably to visit his mother, who I've heard has been sick. Makes me wonder if he's staying here while he's visiting her or if he's making the two-hour drive every day. Seems like four hours in the car would infringe on his stalking abilities." She frowned. "I'm not sure what his endgame was either. Maybe to scare you into submission, but he can't possibly think it would have driven you to him. You two weren't even in a relationship. Unless you were in one in his head. I don't know. It doesn't feel right."

Officer Billy poked his head over the top of his cubicle. "Are you guys talking about Jamie Gagnon?"

"Yes, why?" Micki asked.

"He's here."

"Here? Where?" Savannah said, looking around the police station.

"Not here, here. Like here, in town. I saw him this morning

sitting in traffic on Main. I think his mom is still down with pneumonia."

"Are you sure it was him?" Micki started to pull her jacket off the back of her chair.

"Pretty sure."

"Why didn't you call me? I could have arrested the fucker!"

"On what grounds?"

"Valid point. I'll go pay his mother a little visit and see if he's over there. Where's the mirror?" Micki asked, zipping up her black soft shell jacket.

Savannah sighed and handed over the mirror and the packaging. Micki examined it carefully as though she were looking for an explanation to jump out at her. She handed it over to Billy. "Send this for prints, please."

"Can I see the video?" Savannah clicked her nails on the desk nervously.

Micki nodded. She placed the mirror down gingerly, pulled up the app and forwarded to the appropriate time. "There he is," she said, handing her the phone.

"Ugh, that gives me chills. He's just so…bold. Jamie's always been more sneaky than audacious. I suppose I don't know him as well as I thought."

"Can you tell if it's him?"

"Not really. I guess it could be. It could really be anyone though. The picture isn't clear enough."

"I know, I put a call into SafetyVision. Tell me about this. How do you know it's definitely from Jamie?"

Savannah pointed to the mirror. "This is an almost exact replica of the mirror I have hanging in my office. I think I told you about it? He bought it for me shortly after he started working for me. At the time, I thought it odd, but I knew he was always trying to solidify his place in the office. That was before I knew his…intentions." Savannah shrugged. "It's a lovely piece, so I decided to leave it."

"Yeah," Micki said, staring at the lipstick message. "Something must have triggered him, or he's just been keeping it bottled up all this time, waiting for the right time to strike."

Savannah looked down at the ground. "Shouldn't I feel some sort of relief?"

Micki walked around the desk and gave Savannah's shoulder a light squeeze. "Yes. I should, too. I'm sure once they find him, or once *we* find him and lock him up, we'll calm down. At least now we know who we're looking for."

Nodding, Savannah put her hand over Micki's. "Eliana has that birthday party sleepover tonight at Amelia's house. Are you coming over right from work?"

"I have to send some files over to the Middletown PD, but I should be home shortly after that. Do you want to just stay here with me until it's time to go?"

"No, I'll head home first. Don't worry, I'll set the motion sensor and double-check the windows and doors," Savannah told her, smiling. "I feel a little more in control knowing who is doing this. The little weasel's too afraid to show his face."

"Don't get complacent. He's obviously not playing with a full deck, so we can't underestimate him. We need to be ready."

"And we will be. Do you think it's okay to let Eliana go tonight?"

Micki nodded. "I do. I know Amelia's parents. They volunteered at the bullying awareness seminar we held last year. Very nice people. And all the threats are to do with you. He never mentions El at all."

"Okay. Do you want to pick up the Early Bird for dinner when you're done? I'm not in the mood to cook tonight."

"I could cook for you? An old family dish. I call it SpaghettiOs Surprise," Micki said. She looked at Savannah expectantly.

Savannah swallowed hard. "Sure. That sounds…interesting. Thank you."

"Aww. That was probably the sweetest and most selfless thing you've ever done in your life. Subjecting yourself to a canned dinner. I was joking. I'll pick something up from the Bird."

Savannah rolled her eyes as she pulled her camel coat tightly around her waist. "I'll see you soon."

Light rain tapped against Savannah's windshield. She sat in the parking lot of the police station, listening to the hum of her engine. Her fear had diminished, somewhat, and while she now knew what Jamie was capable of, she had a difficult time seeing him as a threat. He was always so submissive. None of it made any sense.

Fury built up inside Savannah as she replayed the events of the last few weeks, from the flowers to the jack-in-the-box to the intrusion into her home. She would do everything she could to ensure that Jamie didn't get off with some piddly one-year prison sentence for causing the terror that he'd put her and her daughter through.

Savannah closed her eyes and took a breath. She shifted into reverse, trying to get past Jamie's possible motives without shuddering in disgust. Micki was going to come over later, and that put a smile on her face. There was so much wild emotion coursing through her that she decided to focus on just that one, that period of the present, and she'd deal with the rest later.

Still, something felt off. She didn't know what she expected, but she thought she'd feel a mountain fall away from her shoulders. Maybe once he was under arrest, she'd feel better. Savannah pulled out onto the wet road, the streetlights casting hazy halos above her.

CHAPTER TWENTY-THREE

Micki locked the station door behind her, slipping the keys into her front pocket. She was happy that the case was finally wrapping up, but Jamie's motive niggled at her. She had to have missed something about him, but she couldn't figure out exactly what.

She pulled up to 47 Oak Street, a cute little blue house with a black chain-link fence surrounding it. It was small and could have used a paint job, but the yard was neat, and it looked as if the owners did the best they could with what they had. A pink flag attached to the house with tiny birds welcoming spring waved lazily in the early evening breeze. A black sign with bright orange letters warning trespassers to Beware of Dog was attached to the gate.

Micki lifted the latch and entered the yard before freezing immediately. She heard the tinkle of a metal collar get closer and closer. She turned quickly to find a Yorkshire terrier making a beeline for her. The dog was probably a good four pounds after a long soak in the bathtub.

"Hi," Micki said in her best baby voice. The dog sniffed her boot and flopped over on its belly. Micki gave it scratches while she read the tag attached to the collar. Bess.

"Well, hello, Bess. Is your mom home?" Micki scooped her

up, and Bess licked the underside of her chin. Micki rang the doorbell with Bess perched under her arm.

"Yes?" a woman asked, opening the door. "Did Bess get out?"

"No, not at all. She came up to greet me. Mrs. Gagnon, can I talk to you for a minute? Is your son here?"

"Patrick?"

"No, Jamie."

"No, he's not. He left this morning. Come in," she said, standing to the side of the door to allow Micki inside.

Micki put Bess down on the floor, and she ran happily over to her water bowl. Mrs. Gagnon led them into the kitchen where she sat gingerly on one of the wooden chairs. "Is something wrong with Jamie?"

"He's fine, as far I know. I just wanted to ask him a few questions about an issue involving his former employer."

Mrs. Gagnon took a deep breath. "Can't seem to shake this pneumonia," she said, pulling an inhaler out of her housecoat. "Jamie came to see me last night after I asked him to come. I just wasn't feeling right, so I wanted someone close by. He went back to Connecticut this morning. He called me from his work line when he arrived. My son Patrick is on his way here now. He doesn't live far, but it's harder for him to steal away since he has a wife and three sons."

Micki nodded. So, Jamie came to visit his sick mother, and while he was at it, decided to hang around Savannah's backyard and then leave her a replica of the mirror he'd given her with a threatening message on it. Micki couldn't make it fit together. Something was off.

"When was the last time Jamie came to see you? And did he stay in the house with you?"

Mrs. Gagnon went to answer but doubled over in a coughing fit. Micki rubbed her back and handed her a glass of water. If Jamie was the stalker, and he was using his sick mother as a reason to come to town, she hoped he resisted arrest when they caught up with him.

"It's been a few weeks. I thought I was getting better. But he stayed like he always does." She finally got the words out after taking a long drink of water.

"Did Jamie go out anywhere last night? Leave the house for anything?" Micki asked.

"I don't believe so. We watched that millionaire show after dinner, and then I went to bed. He said he was going to as well."

"Does he ever mention his old boss to you? Savannah Castillo?"

Mrs. Gagnon pursed her lips. "Not much. He asks once in a while about the town hall office, things of that nature." She coughed. "But he works for a congresswoman down in Connecticut now, so he's got his hands full with the campaign. Is there a problem with Castillo? Is Jamie in trouble?"

"Nothing you need to worry about. We just think your son might have some information that could help us with an issue we're having. I won't take up any more of your time. Thank you so much for speaking with me," Micki said. She handed her a business card. "Please, give me a call, or have Jamie call me if he shows up unexpectedly. If you're really not feeling well, Urgent Care is open for another hour. Would you like to go?"

Mrs. Gagnon coughed. "No, I'm feeling a bit better. My son will be here soon. Thank you, Chief."

Micki checked her phone to see if the Middletown police had called. Nothing yet.

❖

The Early Bird seemed fairly quiet, although there weren't many parking spots available. Micki parked across the street and heard someone call her name from behind her.

"Mick!"

"Oh, hey, Chloe. I'm so sorry I haven't called since the other day at lunch. Everything has been a blur, seriously."

Chloe nodded. "It's okay, I get it. Have you talked to Rebecca?"

Micki cringed. "No. I was supposed to go home and talk to her, too. She mad?"

"I think she was just pissed off about the whole thing with her dad. She told me that she knew it wasn't your fault but that her dad was kind of her hero, and she didn't even want to think about him doing anything terrible like that. That there was no way he was involved. You don't think he is, do you?"

"Probably not. We got a very important lead tonight, so hopefully, this all ends sooner than later." Micki looked away from Chloe, focusing on a trash can nearby. She didn't want to tell Chloe what a horrible person Gary Raye was. She was afraid Chloe would relay the message to Rebecca, and really, it wasn't her place. Maybe she'd figure it out for herself, maybe not.

"That's awesome. I hope so. We miss having you around. *Real Housewives of Ogunquit* just isn't the same without your commentary. Rebecca asked if I wanted to sublet your room since you're never there anymore."

"You going to the Bird?" Micki asked as they crossed the street in stride. She wasn't about to discuss the idea of her roommate leasing her room without even talking to her.

"Yeah. I can't deal with a can of chicken noodle soup for one more night."

"I'm actually going over there to pick up dinner."

"For you and Savannah?"

Micki was taken aback. "Um…yeah. How did you know?"

"Just a really good guess. You might not be quite as sneaky as you think you are," Chloe said with a smile. "I'm also here to pick up some books from Aunt May. I told her I'd help her with her accounting crap for tax purposes. She'll be in a mood, I'm sure."

Micki smirked. Aunt May was always in a mood. "Oh, I meant to ask you, did David go the Early Bird the other night for pie? When I talked to him the other day, he mentioned seeing you there."

Chloe scrunched up her face in thought. "Yeah, actually he did. Why? The whole Savannah thing?"

"Just wondering. I'm glad you remembered. Clears a few things up." She paused as they made their way onto the Early Bird's patio. "It was still early, right? Like five?"

"I have no idea what time it was. I wasn't...oh wait. No, it couldn't have been five. We didn't get there until after dark. Aunt May only had the tiny pieces left that nobody wanted."

"We?"

"Yeah, it was the weirdest thing. I ran into him at Record Time in the CD section. Of course, we were like the only ones there. Neither of us have moved on to digital yet." Chloe chuckled. "He asked if I was going to the Bird, so after he checked out, we walked back together."

A pit began to form in her stomach. "He didn't mention that. What did he buy?" she asked quietly.

Chloe looked at her as if she had three heads. "Oh, right. You can tell a lot about a dude by his musical interests. And David is obviously a cool guy. He bought *Harvest Moon* by Neil Young."

"Nice."

"Yeah. And some other album called *American Folk Songs for Kids*. Or something like that. Said he'd been feeling nostalgic lately."

Micki took out her phone and pulled up the website for Record Time, looking through their selection of children's albums. She found the album David had purchased.

Track Listing:
1.   Alice the Camel
2.   Buffalo Gals

3. Skip to My Lou
4. You Are My Sunshine
5. She'll Be Coming 'Rou…

Chloe's voice faded into the background while Micki felt a punch to the gut, the wind knocked out of her. She cleared her head and found her voice. Chloe was still talking about the early 90s music scene, seemingly unaware of the change in Micki's demeanor.

"Sorry, Chloe, I have to go."

"Micki?" she called out as Micki turned and ran off.

Micki raced back to her car, unable to breathe or to see straight. If not for the urgency she felt, she would have doubled over from the cramps that invaded her stomach. Just another reason being emotionally involved was such a bad idea. She should have trusted her gut. "Goddamn it. How did I not see it?" She started her engine with trembling hands.

CHAPTER TWENTY-FOUR

Savannah left the bottle of red on the counter to breathe for a few minutes. She pulled down two wineglasses from the shelf and set those down as well. She couldn't get her mind off Jamie, why he was doing this, what outcome he hoped to achieve. She tried to remember instances where he had displayed dangerous behavior or given any inkling that he had such darkness inside of him. She couldn't think of any. He was forward and crass toward the end but never outright threatening. Savannah had never given him any reason to think she was interested in him romantically. He was a good assistant, a *very* good assistant, but that was all there was. It was never going to be anything more. And she hadn't heard anything from him in ages. Why now?

She checked the time again, waiting expectantly for Micki to show up with dinner. Savannah was so pleased to tell Eliana that the bad man was going to be caught and that everything really was going to be okay. When she dropped her off at her friend's house, she noticed Eliana's steps were just a little bit lighter. Jamie, the preppy piece of shit, wouldn't be able to scare them ever again.

Uncertainty still hung over her, but she was confident that Jamie would be caught and charged. Either Micki would find him at his mother's house, or the police department in Connecticut would apprehend him. Savannah's stomach fluttered with anticipation, especially knowing that she and Micki had the house to themselves for the evening. It was almost like a celebration. Even though there was still so much awe surrounding the development of their relationship, Savannah couldn't help but feel the tiniest bit hopeful. It was happening at lightning speed and unpredictably, but it was real. Of that she was confident. Savannah didn't think she'd ever been so sure of *anything*. She was petrified and more than a little curious as to how someone so different from her could bring her to her knees with little more than a look. It just didn't fit the narrative of her life that she had so carefully built. But maybe that was exactly what she needed. To change the narrative and let it flow more naturally.

She poured herself a glass of wine, savoring the full-bodied flavor as it coursed down her throat. She removed her suit jacket and unbuttoned her shirt a little, appreciating the cool air on her chest.

The door finally opened, but the blast of the motion sensor alarm assaulted her senses. "Ah, sorry," she called into the foyer. "I forgot to reset it."

Smiling, Savannah walked into the hallway, where that smile slowly faded. Micki wasn't standing in her doorway. The hooded figure stood staring at her, completely still, threatening. The wineglass slipped from Savannah's fingers, shattering on the tile floor in slow motion. Droplets of wine flew in all different directions, creating tiny puddles of blood-hued liquid: a piece of appalling abstract art she couldn't help but see even as fear engulfed her.

She turned to run, but he was on her before she could gain any distance. He held her tight to his body, a blade pressed into the soft flesh of her neck.

"What do you want?" she choked out, half scream, half sob.

"*You*, Savannah. You haven't figured that out by now?"

The deep voice, accented with a hint of Midwest, swirled in her head like something out of a nightmare. For an instant, she forgot her circumstances and tried to turn her head. "David?" she asked quietly.

"I have to say, I'm a little offended that you were so quick to disregard me as a suspect. Maybe I wasn't the most exciting boyfriend in the world, but I deserve a little credit."

Savannah swallowed hard, the cold metal leaving red lines near her collarbone. "Can we talk about this? David, this doesn't have to go any further. Please, give me a chance."

"I'm fresh out of chances to give you, Savannah. I tried. I left messages, I texted you, I tried to get you to see me. To make you see that what we had wasn't dead, it just needed a little resuscitation from *both* of us. You were unwilling. Now, come with me."

David pushed into the back of her knee with his own, prompting her to move forward. "We don't need to leave, David. We can stay here and talk. If we could just *talk*, you'd see—"

"Your girlfriend will be here any minute, I presume. Can't have that. Now go," he said, pushing her more forcefully this time.

The thought of leaving the house with him poured fresh panic over her, causing her to struggle forcefully in his grasp. "No!"

He gripped the collar of Savannah's shirt, and she heard the silk tear. His forearm tightened against her chest, preventing escape. The knife he held in his hand now brushed threateningly against her breastbone.

"Stop it," David said. His voice was deep and sounded more like a growling animal than the man she had once shared her life with.

Savannah swallowed hard. "I can make this right, David." She quivered, hopelessness clenching at her chest.

"No, Savannah, you can't. Not here, not now."

In a shocking burst of desperation, Savannah brought her fist up behind her, aiming for David's face. She caught him on his cheek, causing him to hiss in pain, but it wasn't enough for him to let go.

"You never did know when to just shut up." He pulled her back by the collar again and slammed her forcefully into the wall, headfirst.

And then everything went black.

❖

Micki burst through the front door, the motion sensor futilely blaring its warning. She switched it off, drew her gun, and looked to the floor. The broken glass and spilled wine stared up at her, admonishing her for being too late. She ran through the house anyway, praying that the scene in the foyer didn't tell the story that she was sure it told.

He had taken her. Or worse. But she wouldn't allow that train of thought to creep in; it would consume her, and Micki needed to keep her head straight. Her heart felt as if it was going to explode in her chest. As she made her way from room to room, images of Savannah reeled through her mind like a movie. She thought of that morning, of Savannah running her hands through her hair, of softly caressing the amber skin leading to her belly button. She thought of how it was when she'd first met Savannah, her seething condescension, the repulsion between them that was just a magnet in disguise. She thought of Eliana holding her mother's hand outside the school, but far enough away that none of her friends would see that she still clutched on to her mother for support. She thought of sitting across from her at dinner, herself and Eliana forming a mutiny against Savannah's perpetually healthy offerings. Micki shook her head. *Stop acting like she's dead.* There was no option. She had to find her, she had to save her, and she had to make him pay.

Micki called the station. Jack answered. "Shaw set up the assistant, Jack. It was him after all. Get me his address and put out an APB. I'm pretty sure she's been kidnapped. Have Billy sweep the town, get his last known whereabouts. And then I want a copy of the license and credit card he used to check into that fucking Caribbean hotel."

She hung up and punched David's address into the GPS on her phone, activated her siren and lights, and prayed that she'd get lucky.

CHAPTER TWENTY-FIVE

Savannah slowly swam to the surface, sucking in oxygen as though she had been drowning. She looked out of blurry eyes to find her hands clasped together with zip ties. She tried to kick her foot only to feel the resistance of being tied to a chair. She raised her head slowly to look around the room, dizziness threatening to bathe her in darkness again.

She didn't know this place. She was in what appeared to be a bedroom. The walls were paneled with dark cedar. Exposed beams ran up the walls and over the ceiling. She was sitting on a plush avocado green wing-back with dark wood trim. It had probably been comfortable back in the seventies. It was dark out, that much she could tell. The windows had no curtains, but there was nothing there for Savannah to see. Just a wall of blackness through every window she could turn to.

"So glad you've finally decided to join me, sunshine," David said, grinning widely. He walked in and sat on the edge of a bed a few feet away from her, made up with a deep plaid comforter and matching pillows.

"Where are we?" she groaned, her voice thick and heavy.

"Away. I told you about this cabin. More than once. You never did want to come up here with me. I told you how romantic and secluded it was. You told me it sounded too much like camping. Shame. Now, even if you did escape, you'd never find your way home." David shrugged as if they were just having a regular conversation between friends.

"Why are you doing this?"

"Ah, the inevitable 'why.' Why do we do anything, Savannah? Why did you leave me when we had a perfect relationship? I was going to propose to you, you know. We could have had a beautiful wedding. Which, of course, would lead to little Davids and little Savannahs running through the house. We could have had it all." David looked down at Savannah with what seemed like pity.

"How did you get in my house?"

"I had a key made. Remember the time you let me borrow your car when mine was in for service? I figured I'd surprise you at some point. Let myself in and make you a romantic dinner. Something like that. But you never gave me the opportunity. You ruined it."

"We had the locks changed."

"I wasn't dumb enough to get a copy of the front door key. People change those locks all the time. I got a copy of your bulkhead key." He held up a squat key with a black and yellow rubber key cover.

Savannah cleared her throat, her mouth dry and sore. "You accepted it at the time. You told me that you understood how I felt, and even though you didn't want it to end, you just wanted me to be happy."

David's friendly demeanor morphed into one of rage. "Well...I *lied*!" he yelled, bending down so their faces were close. "I never *accepted* it, Savannah. But what was I supposed to do?" His casual manner returned, and he smiled faintly again. "Was I supposed to tell you that I'd see us both dead before I'd see you with another man? Or woman, as the case may be. I've seen you tear people apart limb from limb. I had to tread carefully or I'd end up with a restraining order against me. The more I think about it, this might actually be for the best. No distractions, nothing in our way. The chief was a surprise, definitely didn't see that one coming. Your precocious little daughter can live happily ever after with her new *stepmother*, or whatever the hell she is, and you and I can ride off into the proverbial sunset," he said, shrugging off his sweatshirt and laying it on the bed.

Venom seethed from Savannah's pores. She tugged against the nylon plastic with every ounce of strength she could muster, only to be refused release.

David smiled down at her again. "Hit a nerve, did I?"

"You son of a bitch," she spat. "If I'm riding off into the sunset with *anyone*, I can assure you it'll be in a Winter Valley squad car."

David was on her again before she could even finish the words. He grabbed Savannah by the back of the neck, hard. "Don't test me, Savannah," he said through clenched teeth. "You will *never* love her. More importantly, she will *never* love you. I'm it, Savannah. Your last chance. Everyone knows what a vile bitch you are, stuck up and patronizing. I'm the only one that can see below the surface. The wretched, broken—but so very beautiful—surface. I can make you happy, Savannah."

She looked at his eyes, once so docile, now enflamed. Perhaps another tactic might be necessary. Savannah tried to put forth an air of regret.

"Maybe you're right, David," she admitted, nodding thoughtfully. "Maybe I shouldn't have been so quick to end our relationship. I've always been so sure of myself and so sure of the people in my life. Not that there have been many. Maybe I pushed you away because I was afraid you were getting too close."

David scoffed. "Please. If you think that I believe you now, you're quite naïve, my love. You threw me away because you didn't think I was good enough for you. What you didn't realize was that I was *too* good for you. You may not see it now, but I'll prove it to you. In any way I have to."

"We had some good times together, David. I haven't forgotten. Maybe we could try recreating some of those. We had a lovely time at that little beach getaway a few summers ago."

"You were on your laptop almost the entire time."

"Well, the Fourth of July block party was right around the corner and I had to—you know what? I concede your point. I should have paid more attention to us that weekend." Savannah's stomach rolled at the words coming out of her mouth, but she'd play whatever game she needed to in order to get back to her daughter. And to Micki. "What about the wedding you brought me to in upstate New York? Was it your cousin?"

"It was my sister's wedding. You sat at the table the whole time and complained about the food."

For a brief second, Savannah wondered, *Am I really that unpleasant?* "I have to ask you, then, what is it that you're hoping for here? You don't seem to look fondly on our past together."

"That's just it, Savannah. You never gave yourself to me, not fully. There was always something more pressing, more interesting, someone needier. The only way I could really get you to see *me* was to take you away from all of those distractions. So, here we are."

"Have you ever done this kind of thing before, David?"

"What are you asking?"

"I just, I don't know, I didn't think that kidnapping was something I needed to worry about when we were together." Savannah knew she should keep to the script, give him what he wanted. But her confusion was demanding answers. Did he just snap? Was he a sociopath who knew how to hide it really, really well?

"Don't be ridiculous. I haven't *kidnapped* you. I'm just forcing you to look at something that you wouldn't see without a little bit of prodding. You don't need to be so dramatic. I'd thought about you for years before I worked up the nerve to ask you out. The day you asked me to hand you a stirrer at Cuppa Joe's, I knew you were the one. And then you blew it."

He walked over to her chair, deliberately, and ran his fingers down the length of her hair. Savannah braced herself. Was David going to kill her? She hadn't given much thought to her own death but wondered if maybe she should have. Eliana would have to go live with her mother, a woman she barely knew. There was so much Savannah wished she had done differently. She shouldn't have isolated herself and Eliana as much as she had. She should have given people the benefit of the doubt. She should have given Micki a chance before completely writing her off as an imbecile who would ruin the town she'd worked so hard for. She should have allowed herself to take risks, and she should have eaten the damn ice cream. Savannah closed her eyes and prayed for more time.

CHAPTER TWENTY-SIX

The brakes on the Crown Vic squelched as she pulled into her designated parking spot at her apartment. Her car was taking up that spot and probably the one next to it, too. She dared someone to give her shit about it.

Rebecca was sitting at the kitchen table, chips and dip set out in front of her. She was munching lazily while watching videos on her phone.

"What's the matter?" she asked, standing up as soon as Micki walked through the door. Micki raced through the kitchen toward her bedroom.

"Savannah's missing. He's got her, wherever he is."

"Who, her old assistant?"

"No, David."

"*David?* No! How do you know?"

"I just do. How much do you know about him?"

Rebecca paused. "Oh my God. Not much, really. I've talked to him a few times at the diner, but that's about it. We mostly talk about regular stuff like the food at the diner, weather, his job. That's it, I guess."

"Never about Savannah?"

"No, not at all. He knows I watch her daughter. That would just be weird. Although I guess it might be weird that he's never asked about El, since he was with Savannah for a while."

"Has he ever mentioned anything to you about where he used to live or where he likes to vacation or if he has a secret passage in his house, for God's sake?" Micki rubbed the back of her neck anxiously. She was headed to his house when she thought about the fact that she didn't have enough ammo if things went to shit.

"No, nothing like that. I'm really sorry, Mick. I don't know anything about him in that way."

"Does he have any family? Any fucking friends around here?"

"I'm pretty sure his family lives out in Iowa. Friends? Maybe bank people? He's kind of a loner. Which is surprising because he's a good-looking guy who can be really friendly."

Micki breathed out slowly. "Okay. Thanks. If you don't hear from me, can you please pick up Eliana from Amelia Haggerty's house at nine tomorrow morning? Just tell her Savannah had an emergency business meeting or something."

"Wouldn't she expect you?"

Micki nodded. "Yeah, I suppose she would. Tell her I had to go with her mom. There's some sort of meeting in Manchester that we needed to go to."

"Okay, no problem. Call me as soon as you know anything. Are you and Savannah like, together now?"

"Rebecca, this is really not the time." Micki ran to her closet and grabbed the metal box containing her backup pistol and ammunition.

Rebecca followed her in. "I totally get that. Yes or no question."

"I don't know. Kind of. I have to go," Micki said, flying out the door and down the steps to the parking lot.

"Are you there yet?" Micki asked, keeping the button pressed on her radio as she jumped into her car.

"Doesn't look like he's here. I'm canvassing the perimeter at the moment. SUV isn't in the driveway," Jack said, his voice coming in clear through the low hum of static.

"I'm on my way." Micki rubbed the bridge of her nose and pressed down hard on the worn gas pedal.

❖

She kicked the door to his small, ranch-style house so hard that it swung from the hinges. Micki's weapon was steady as she searched David's house for any signs of life. There was nothing. Angrily, she tore through closets and flipped tables onto their sides, spilling the contents onto the floor. She searched for something, anything, that could tell her where he had taken Savannah.

"Fuck!" she yelled into the empty house, going through each room, corner by corner. She took a few deep breaths to slow herself down. Micki had to be thorough, methodical. She radioed Billy and directed him to get any records he could find—registrations, deeds, warrants—anything.

Micki searched through the shoeboxes David had stacked on the shelf in his closet. Bank receipts, invoices, the mortgage documents for the house she was currently ransacking. She moved to his nightstand and found a to-do list, a phone number for a podiatrist, and the operating instructions for a scientific calculator. It was all very normal. There was no sign of a detailed diary written in blood with a quill, outlining David's innermost thoughts and plans, though Micki really wished there was. For a horrifying second, she wondered if she might have been wrong about him.

But no. She knew Jamie had been too easy, too blatant. Her gut was never at peace with Jamie as the villain. He was sleazy and abhorrent, but by everything she had uncovered, not an overt criminal. And then there was that song, that *fucking* song that was too obscure to be a coincidence. If David had children or had even purchased the Johnny Cash version, it would have given Micki pause. But he didn't. She wasn't wrong, not this time. She could feel it in her bones.

David lived a pretty nondescript life. He had orange juice in the refrigerator, a *Time* magazine on his coffee table, a painting of the ocean at dusk hanging on his wall. There was nothing that screamed out that this man was unhinged. Micki slid a small Tupperware container from beneath his bed, and for a moment, thought she had hit pay dirt.

She peeled off the lid to find pictures of Savannah, some alone, some with David. Micki's stomach flipped with anger and fear at the sight of her. They both looked happy enough. In a few photos, they were dressed up and posed at some function; in some, David had taken selfies on the lake. Savannah's lips were turned up in a smile, but that glimmer that Micki had grown so fond of was missing. Other than the photos, a newspaper article detailing Savannah's acquisition of the elementary school property and a necklace with a sterling silver sun lay on the bottom of the container. That was it.

"Is everything all right?" a voice asked, interrupting Micki's pursuit.

"Who's there?" Micki asked, jumping up and running toward the foyer. Her hand immediately went to her weapon.

"Ruth Davis!" the tall woman answered quickly.

Micki assessed that she was probably in her late sixties and seemed harmless enough. Her oversized, retro glasses probably helped with that.

"I'm David's neighbor. I thought I heard some commotion so I wanted to make sure he was okay. You're the police chief."

"Do you know where he is?" Micki asked, trying to appear more relaxed than she felt.

The woman's eyes moved over the mess Micki had made. "Um, no, I don't. He hasn't been around much lately. He's a very nice man, though. Never had any problems here."

"Has he mentioned anything about a girlfriend? Or any place that he goes regularly besides Winter Valley? Does he visit his family often?"

"Well, I don't talk to him all that much. More so during the summertime because our decks are quite close. If you take a look through his kitchen window, you can see where our backyards intersect. He's usually grilling—"

"That's so nice, that the two of you share stories in the summer," Micki interrupted, forcefully tucking a piece of hair behind her ear. "So, has he? Mentioned anything about a girlfriend or anywhere that he goes often?"

Ruth Davis looked rattled. "He was dating someone for a while. That Savannah Castillo. From the town council. Not the nicest woman, *that* I can tell you." She raised her eyebrows at Micki, sharing a secret with her. "She has quite the reputation for putting people off."

"I'm familiar with Ms. Castillo, thank you," Micki said, interrupting again. "What about a vacation home or a rental or something like that? Does he like to camp? Does he like to hike? Does he go to the ocean much?"

Ruth Davis thought carefully, her finger on her chin. "Is this official police business?"

"Yes."

She nodded as though that made some kind of difference. "He did mention that his father had a cabin somewhere up north. I'm not sure where, exactly. He was very private, David."

Micki's pulse quickened. She continued to half listen as Ruth Davis prattled on about the neighborhood and how they all took turns hosting the summer barbecue and that this year it was David's turn, so she hoped he'd be able to fulfill his end of the bargain; otherwise, that would just be rude. Micki looked through the drawers on the table in his hallway, sorting through checkbooks and writing utensils and key chains from various tourist attractions. And then she found it.

A forwarded piece of mail from an address she wasn't familiar with: 44 Rural Route 9, Sunshine Point, ME. It was postmarked 2014, some kind of tax notice. It wasn't rock solid, by any means, but it could hold the key to Savannah's whereabouts. It was the best lead she had. She thanked Ruth Davis for her time and ran out the door.

"Me again, Billy. Can you tell me who owns this property?" Micki rattled off the address, even though she was already getting on the highway. She wasn't going to waste a second if that's where he had her. She could hear Billy typing in the query.

"Yup. That belongs to David Shaw Senior. Who, coincidentally, checked into the resort last week down in Jamaica. I have the records here if you want them. Looks like neither of them use a suffix in their everyday life."

"Son of a bitch. What else do you have?"

"Not much. He mortgages the house here in town, leases his Ford, never been married, his family members are mostly living in Iowa. Not a whole lot here."

"I'm on my way up to the cabin now," Micki said. "Call in some backup, will you?"

CHAPTER TWENTY-SEVEN

Savannah remembered what David's fingers felt like on her skin not so very long ago. A cup of vanilla. Fine. Nice, even. But nothing exciting. She tried to will herself back to that place now as his hand caressed her arm. It felt like an earthworm slithering slowly up toward her shoulder, but she swallowed her revulsion. Shuddering in disgust wouldn't do. Not now.

He smiled down at her with what appeared to be pity or, worse, sympathy. Savannah watched as he walked out of the room, his hand worrying the unusual five o'clock shadow that had grown in. He had on a blue T-shirt with one of those happy-faced stick figures on it. Savannah remembered it from their time together. She couldn't come to terms with the idea that this was the same man who watched late-night talk shows while eating peanuts out of a tin. The same man that offered to have the tires on her Infiniti rotated. She didn't end the relationship because he was a bad man or because he treated her poorly. Savannah just decided that she wanted more. More what? She hadn't known, exactly. Until she felt it with Micki.

"We really could try again," she attempted, taking a deep breath. David sat on the edge of the bed again, taking a long swallow of hard lemonade. "I won't lie. You've scared me half to death. But maybe it was just what I needed to finally realize the truth. I was unfair to you."

For an instant, Savannah saw David's face soften. His eyes let go of some of the anger, and he seemed to be contemplating her honesty. "I could never trust you again, Savannah. I would have done anything for you, and you just walked away. Like I was nothing."

Savannah searched within herself to see if there was truth in what David was saying. Had she just cast him aside like he was garbage? No. No, she hadn't. She'd told him the truth. There were many, *many* things Savannah regretted in her lifetime; the way she and David had split up was not one of them.

"Untie me. I'll show you how sorry I am." Savannah sighed internally, knowing her options were limited. She wanted to spit venom at him, to tell him that she was under no obligation to return *anyone*'s feelings, and his supposed undying love for her was his problem, not hers. But now wasn't the time for that particular speech.

David stood over her. She looked up at him beneath hooded lids. She pulled her bottom lip between her teeth, hoping she was the very picture of sorrow and repentance. He was wavering, she could feel it.

"So you can try to run? You obviously take me for a fool. I can see nothing has changed."

"Where would I go? Where would I even run to? I have no phone, no car, and you've said that there isn't a neighbor for miles. Running through the woods at night isn't exactly my idea of a good time. It's just…my wrists hurt. I'm tired. And I want to make this right. David, please. Like you said before, it's just the two of us, no distractions. We can talk and maybe reconnect." Savannah looked at him hopefully, choking down the bile that threatened to crawl up her throat.

David paused. His stick person T-shirt was starting to show signs of perspiration. He leaned down and pressed his forehead against Savannah's. "If I free you and you so much as try to go to the bathroom without my permission, I will hogtie you, gag you, and leave you for dead. Do you understand me?" His breath was hot against her face.

"Yes." Savannah was breathless. She felt a sliver of hope begin to creep in.

David produced a pocket knife and made quick work of the zip ties. He stared down at Savannah with a mix of anticipation and mistrust. "Get on the bed."

Savannah rubbed her wrists and stretched her arms; rolled her neck to ease the ache. She had no idea how much time had passed since he'd taken her to this godforsaken place. She gingerly got out of the chair and made her way to the bed. Savannah willed away the tears that desperately wanted to fall and sat down on the edge of the plaid comforter. David motioned for her to get closer to the center, which she did. He sat next to her, their thighs touching. He fidgeted with his pocket knife.

"I didn't want it to be like this, Savannah. If you had only listened to me. If you had only put the same amount of effort into our relationship that you put into ending it. You did this."

Everything inside of her wanted to scream, hit, strangle. His misguided manipulation was disgusting.

"And I said I was sorry," she whispered.

David put his hand on her back, tenderly. Savannah tensed immediately.

"Sore," she explained when he frowned at her. She played with a tiny piece of filling sticking up through the fabric and looked around the room as casually as possible, trying to locate anything that could be used as a weapon. She had to do something, and she had to do it quick before she found herself tied to the chair again.

"I am sorry about that," David said, resting his hand on Savannah's knee. "I'll be honest. It was gratifying watching you, watching your fear grow. Even though it led to that woman staying over at your house. At first, I was happy about it. I was having enough of an impact on you for you to alter your entire life. But then, when I saw the two of you, I was disgusted. I knew you'd been with women before, obviously, but to let her take advantage of you like that. It's weak, Savannah. Weak. I knew sending you that stupid mirror would send the chief scurrying in the wrong direction. I always hated that Jamie gave you something you kept on the wall, like he meant something to you. It seemed fitting he be the one you thought was lovesick."

So many things ran through her head. Explanations, curses, insults. Cutting people to their core had always been something that Savannah was deft at. That she wasn't able to do it to David made her sick to her stomach. She knew she could reduce him to an amoeba in under a minute, but sharp words weren't going to help now. She needed to *think.*

David took her arm and pulled her closer to him. He leaned forward, rubbing his thumb along the line of her eyebrow. "I've missed this so much," he said, tilting forward to kiss her.

Savannah lay there, allowing him to brush her lips with his. The tickle of his beard and the roughness of his fingertips nearly sent her into a panic, but she persisted. She parted her lips slowly, waiting for him to do the same.

David responded instantly. He opened his mouth, inching closer to Savannah. Groans of his approval began to fill the room.

Until Savannah took his bottom lip into her mouth, sucking gently. And then she bit down. *Hard.*

CHAPTER TWENTY-EIGHT

Of course it would rain. Finding a house or cabin or a fucking *tent* on some dirt-covered rural route in deep, dark Maine in blinding rain should be a piece of cake.

"Where the fuck is 202?" Micki shouted, squinting to see the miniscule road signs up ahead. They weren't even signs, really, just small plastic placards stuck into the side of the road on flimsy stakes. She cursed herself for not investing in an old-school Garmin or TomTom for the cruiser, considering she'd lost her cell signal an hour earlier. At some point she'd have to persuade the council to budget for a new vehicle; the urgency just hadn't been there before. Micki resorted to the freshly coffee-stained map of Maine she'd thankfully grabbed at the New Hampshire line Gas 'n Go. She hadn't seen a house or a street light in probably forty miles. The dampened map and instinct alone would need to drive this one.

The Sunshine Point Police Department, which was run solely on a volunteer basis, was attending their town meeting to select the new animal control officer. Micki explained the urgent nature of her request. The very nice but entirely unhelpful receptionist told Micki that she would have someone contact her just as soon as the meeting was over. Shouldn't be too long now.

The rain fell in sheets. The cruiser's worn wipers battled their way through as best they could, but visibility was mediocre at best. Micki could barely make out the lines of the road, but she was able to notice something sauntering across before she slammed into it. Squelching her brakes, she squinted again, and yes, it really was a black bear crossing the single-lane pavement into the woods on the opposite side. He looked offended by her presence before he picked up the pace and disappeared into the brush. Micki rubbed her temples.

How far away *was* this place? She felt as if she'd been driving for three, four hours at least. The clock on her dashboard proved her wrong. She'd only been on the road for an hour and fifty-three minutes.

Micki tried to call into the station but found she was in yet another dead zone. Even the crackle of her radio kept cutting out.

Her headlights illuminated a drooping sign propped up against a rusted guard rail. Rural Route 7. She was almost there, finally. An unseen gully in the road caused her tire to dip down, rocking her car as if she was in the middle of an earthquake. *No, no, no. No car trouble now. I need to get to her.*

The road became nearly impassable the closer to Route 9 she got. Micki looked down at her speedometer and saw that she had slowed to less than ten miles per hour, and even that felt too fast. What purpose could any human being have for a vacation home this far into the woods? Unless the plan was to kidnap and kill someone without anyone finding out. The nearest supermarket was probably thirty miles away, at least. There would be no fulfilling a late-night craving for mint chocolate chip, that was for sure.

After what seemed like another hour sputtering down the unpaved road, Micki quickly flicked off her headlights. In the distance, she could see a faint light in what appeared to be a window. A low-hanging tree branch scraped the hood of her car, startling her. She hadn't realized just how complacent she'd become in the banal requirements of her small police force.

Micki pulled over about a hundred feet from the house. It was eerily quiet this far away from civilization. She didn't even hear any crunching leaves or scurrying. The only sound was Micki's own breathing and the pounding of the rain against the car. She got out and crept alongside her vehicle until she found what she was looking for. A newer-model burgundy Explorer sat in the mock driveway, which was really just a clearing of brush on the packed dirt. David's SUV. That meant that Savannah had to be inside. She had to be.

Crouching down, Micki walked slowly toward the side of the house, constantly wiping rain from her eyes. She was careful to keep the sound of her footsteps to a minimum. Alerting David to the fact that she was outside would be catastrophic.

Gratefulness washed over Micki when she saw a dirty basement window below one of the side windows. She had no idea what she would be facing, but she'd shot up a silent prayer that David's father's cabin or tiny home or waterfront cottage or whatever the hell it was would have underground access and not a slab. She appreciated the small victory.

The house was still silent. Micki wasn't sure if that was a good thing or not. Better than screaming, she supposed, but on the other hand, screaming would have at least informed her of their whereabouts. Of their...aliveness. She shook her head and commanded herself to think positively. David wouldn't have gone through all of that trouble just to kill Savannah five minutes after he had her where he wanted her.

Micki shook the latch on the window only to find it wouldn't budge. Unsurprising. She slid her brand-new pair of glass cutters out of her coat pocket and went to work. At least the police station had had *some* foresight that a crime could actually take place, even if it wasn't the norm.

She jammed the tool against the glass and cut in a circle near the top of the window, just enough to fit her wrist through the opening. Micki hadn't done this before on glass quite so thick, so it wasn't popping out as quickly as she had hoped. She cut over the same indents she had already made and pushed the toe of her boot to the center of the circle. She pushed, hard, harder, and then finally heard a soft crack. The circle pushed through, to Micki's horror, as she thought it was going to sail to the ground and shatter into little bits. She stuck her wrist through and felt for it, relieved to find that it was still hanging on by a tiny thread of glass. She yanked it off and undid the latch with her thumb.

The basement was dark. Really, really, dark. Micki crawled through the open window. Her holster caught on the ledge, scraping its way down to rest again on her hip. She grimaced, waiting to hear commotion ensue. It didn't.

She felt her way along the damp stone wall, pushing all thoughts of what she might run into down there aside. She wasn't afraid of a psychopath, but she sure as shit *was* afraid of centipedes.

Rather than use her ultra-bright flashlight to alert everyone within a three-mile radius to her location, Micki pressed the home button on her phone to use the dim light of her lock screen. It was eerie, how little of the room she could see, but maybe that was for the best. She just needed to get Savannah and get the hell out of there.

And then came the deep, masculine shout from above her head. Micki held up her phone and ran toward the stairs.

SECRETS IN A SMALL TOWN

CHAPTER TWENTY-NINE

David tried to pull his head back swiftly once the burn of Savannah's teeth had set in, but Savannah only strengthened her grip. She held on until she felt the unpleasant metallic taste rush over his mouth. She brought her knee up, delivering a crippling blow to his stomach. David gasped for air, blood dripping from his torn lip.

"*Savannah!*" he screamed as she fled the bedroom.

The knob on the front door wouldn't budge. The double-keyed dead bolt that locked from the inside as well as the outside had clearly been recently installed. *Fuck.* She grabbed a lamp from a side table near the coat rack and was just about to smash the window when he rushed at her. Savannah tried to adjust herself to hit David instead of the window, the metal base promising a crucial blow if she could land it, but he had the advantage of home field. David wrested the fixture out of her hand where it fell to the floor with a weak clang.

"You lying bitch," he said to her, knocking her to the ground and then straddling her. He had her hands above her head, his grip too strong for her to break free.

It killed Savannah knowing that he outmatched her on brute strength alone. She was unable to get any traction with her legs because of his size. Savannah felt terror begin to stream through her veins. His eyes were emotionless. His muscles tightened and flexed with every breath.

He spoke through gritted teeth, red spittle flying in every direction. "I will fucking kill you," he said, gravelly and slow, and Savannah believed him.

She thought of Eliana. How she'd never get to see her drive a car or go to college or fall in love. She thought of her mother, who would blame the Almighty for taking everything she loved from her, who would hold on to soul-crushing regret for their fractured relationship. She thought of Micki, who'd made her feel as if she could love again, who'd made her believe she had the ability to make someone else happy. All of it ripped away from her. By a year-long mistake that she didn't even realize she was making.

"I will fucking kill you," he said again, adjusting his grip on the pocket knife he held.

"No. You won't."

Savannah watched as Micki cocked the hammer and readied her weapon, pressing it forcefully against the back of David's neck.

"Get the fuck off her, asshole."

David sneered, letting go of Savannah slowly. He sat back on his heels while Savannah scooted away, sobbing with relief.

"So, the white knight has come to rescue the princess. How novel."

Micki detached her handcuffs from her belt, looking at Savannah. "You okay?"

David used the fraction-of-a-second distraction to swing his arm backward, the corner of his elbow connecting with the center of Micki's stomach.

"No!" Savannah yelled, scrambling to her feet.

It was too late. David was up.

Micki staggered backward, fighting for air. She pointed her gun at David's back just as he turned the corner. "Stay here!" she yelled to Savannah.

For a second, Micki thought she might throw up from the force of David's blow to her stomach. It pulsed with pain. She took off after David, berating herself for giving him the opportunity. It was a rookie move, one she never should have made. She slowed her steps as she entered the bedroom. A closet door was open just a crack.

Micki aimed her gun at the closet door and walked softly toward it. He had the element of surprise on his side, which she had foolishly given up.

His hand shot out from under the bed like a bullet, latching on to Micki's ankle. He pulled hard, and she collapsed to the floor.

David crawled out from under the bed on the opposite side. Micki reached for his leg but only managed to grab a handful of pants.

"He's coming!" Micki shouted to Savannah. She felt panic set in that David would take her hostage again, and Micki would have no other option but to let him go.

Micki scrambled to her feet and heard David's voice from the other room. "Looks like your hero fizzled out on you."

David lunged at Savannah, but she was ready. One straight punch to the underside of David's jaw sent him reeling. He arched backward, his momentum biting back on him like a broken elastic. Micki stood behind him as he fell into her waiting arms. She forced him to his knees with a chokehold fueled by adrenaline and anger.

Savannah nodded. She pushed messy strands of hair away from her forehead, looking down at David in his compromised position, her expression flooded with contempt. "I would rather light myself on fire than 'reconnect' with you. Just so there's no confusion."

"I never should have listened to a cunt like you—"

David shouted in agony as Micki's knee lodged into his spine, splaying him out on his stomach. She locked a cuff around each wrist but kept her knee in place, grinding a little harder than she needed to. "What was that you called her? I must have misheard."

A knock sounded loudly on the door. Micki and Savannah looked at each other in confusion. Micki stood, keeping one heel of her boot on David's back and her gun still pointed at his head and nodded to Savannah to answer the door.

"Sunshine Point Volunteer Police." A small, frail octogenarian greeted her, tipping his hat. "I'm here to see about a possible kidnapping?"

CHAPTER THIRTY

Micki stood against the squad car, her arm draped tightly over Savannah's shoulders. Savannah's head was cradled against her neck as they watched the Sunshine Point Volunteer Police load David into the back of an antique Monte Carlo, a lone blue light stuck haphazardly to the roof of the car. The wind was light and cool, but neither of them felt the chill.

"How did you find me?"

"Fate," Micki sighed, chuckling softly. "CDs and Ruth Davis."

Savannah looked up at her, confused.

"I wish I could have gotten here sooner. I'm so sorry he did this to you."

Savannah wrapped her arms around Micki's waist and squeezed tightly. "I really think he might have killed me, Micki. If you hadn't shown up when you did…" She trailed off, a shiver coursing through her. "I never would have suspected him. Never."

"Maybe he just snapped. It happens, I guess."

"He was always so eager to please and never really showed an angry side. Even when we argued. It was boring, quite frankly. Imagine if I'd known what he was capable of."

"You find someone *not* arguing with you boring? I don't believe it. Ow." Micki laughed as Savannah pinched her side. "How did David know about the mirror?"

"I told him the story while we were dating. He wanted me to get rid of the mirror, but I told him absolutely not. I liked it, so I didn't see any reason to take it down. It was smart of him, really." She paused. "How did you get in? David's key unlocked the door from the outside *and* the inside."

"The basement. Remember, I'm skilled at this sort of thing."

"And for that, I'll be forever grateful."

Micki nodded, breathing in deeply.

"We should get home. When Eliana comes back in the morning, we can tell her it's really, truly over. She doesn't know what's going on, right?"

Micki shook her head. "No. I talked to Rebecca; she was going to pick her up in the morning if I needed her to. But I told her to just wait for word from me and me only before doing anything."

"Good."

"Okay. Let's go."

Savannah looked up at her with a cocked eyebrow. "What's wrong?"

Micki wondered if her cautious tone gave her away. "Nothing! Nothing, I'm just glad you're safe." Micki squeezed Savannah's hand before opening the passenger side door for her.

"Tell me or I'm not getting in the car."

Micki groaned at the starless night sky, though it had mercifully stopped raining. "It's *really* not the time. We can talk about it tomorrow. You were just completely traumatized. You could have been killed. It can wait, I promise you."

"Tell me now."

Micki closed her eyes. Her self-doubt had chosen a fine time to make its presence known. Of all the selfish, ridiculous, childish things to bring up with someone who had just faced a literal madman. "Okay. It's over, thank God. We can live normal lives again without being in constant fear. And I assume this means I'll be moving back into my apartment full-time. Which is totally fine, of course, but…"

"Why?"

"Why what?"

"Why would you move back into your apartment?"

Micki swallowed. "I mean, it's pretty presumptuous, don't you think? We're still kind of figuring out what this is between us, and I don't want to ruin it by being there all the time. You'll get sick of me." She smiled, only half joking. "I just figured you would want me to move back to my apartment so you can get your life back to normal."

Savannah nodded. "Mmm-hmm. Well, obviously you can if that's what you want to do. But please don't move out on my account. I'm fairly certain I'm in love with you."

"The guest room is super nice, and it's fine for...what?" Micki snapped her eyes back up to meet Savannah's.

Savannah nodded again and took Micki's hand in both of her own. "I'm in love with you, Micki. And I want you to stay."

"You...think you're in love with me?" Micki asked, incredulous.

"I do."

"Are you sure you're not saying that because you were just face-to-face with a psychopath?"

Savannah closed her eyes and shook her head but still clasped Micki's hand tightly. "Stop. I love you. I loved you this morning, and I'll love you when we go to sleep tonight. It's not *because* of anything. Just you. You're infuriating and absurd and good-hearted and ridiculously beautiful, and you make me feel whole. I didn't even know that there was anything missing until the moment that you dropped your duffel bag in my foyer. It's all too fast, and I don't know how it happened. But yes, Micki, I love you."

Surprise flooded Micki's chest. A slow smile broke out on her face, and she lunged forward, bringing Savannah taut against her chest. "I can't even tell you how happy I am. I feel the same way, and it doesn't even make sense, I mean, it's not *logical*, like, at all, but I'm so head over heels in love with you, and yes,

I want to be with you and Eliana. I've never felt like this with *anyone*, so I'm really fucking scared, but I don't even care about that right now."

Savannah laughed, holding on to Micki, and fire crackled between them with nothing needed to stoke it. "Can you take me home now? I did just face death, you know."

"Yes, of course. Here," Micki said. She opened the passenger door once more. "Hop in. I love you." She smiled again, just testing the words on her lips to see if they felt right actually being spoken into the blackness of the universe. And yes. Yes, they did.

CHAPTER THIRTY-ONE

They could have found a hotel for the night, but Savannah really just wanted to go home. They didn't pull into the driveway on Kensington Road until the sky was just transforming into a lighter shade of blue.

As they walked toward the front door, Micki put her hand on the small of Savannah's back. "The next few days are going to be daunting. We'll be brought in for questioning, meetings, the bail hearing, etc. Hopefully, they'll send him to Portland. We should probably talk about all the things we're going to need to do."

Savannah gasped at the dried wine stains on her tile floor, shards of glass glittering in the soft light of the overhead. Micki's eyes widened.

"I'll clean it up," she said, bending over to grab the larger pieces of glass.

"No, Micki, it's fine. I just…forgot, I guess. It feels like it's been a hell of a lot longer than…however long it's been. We can deal with it in the morning. Please, let's just go to bed."

The pleading in Savannah's voice nearly broke Micki's heart; she threw the glass she had picked up into the trash and agreed to leave the rest until morning. She took Savannah's hand and led her up the stairs.

"I'm sure you're exhausted." Micki pulled on a faded T-shirt, kicked off her jeans, and searched for an elastic band to put her hair up. "Are you okay to sleep? Do you want to talk or watch some TV or something?"

Micki felt herself pushed up against the dresser, the hard edge of the wood pressing into her lower back. Savannah was in front of her, already completely undressed, running her hands up and down the length of Micki's torso.

"No, I'm not okay to sleep," she whispered, kissing her way softly up Micki's neckline to her earlobe. "But I don't want to talk."

Micki groaned. Her eyelids fluttered closed. "It's been a harrowing day, to say the least. We can just—oh, oh—are you sure?" Micki gasped as the warmth of Savannah's tongue made its way around the shell of her ear.

"Quite sure. I need to touch you, I need you inside me, I need you to make me feel safe again. The way that only you can."

Micki didn't need an engraved invitation. She dropped her head to kiss Savannah's collarbone, letting her hands slide all over her naked body. She could feel the desire within rising at an alarming rate, and she gently pushed Savannah back toward the bed.

Savannah scooted up toward the headboard, cushioning her head with the pillow beneath. She made no move to cover herself, lying in front of Micki completely exposed. A plea in her eyes.

A surge of rage bubbled through Micki's chest, watching Savannah present herself to her, so vulnerable, so open. Right then, arrest didn't feel like enough. Jail didn't feel like enough. Micki wanted David dead.

Sensing her hesitancy, Savannah pulled Micki down on top of her, dragging her T-shirt slowly over her head and tossing it to the floor. "It's okay," she said, wiping the tear away from Micki's cheek. "I'm okay."

Micki smiled bitterly, ashamed that Savannah was the one comforting her. "I'm sorry."

"Don't. You saved me." Savannah brought her hands up to

the sides of Micki's face. "And I hope I can spend the rest of my life returning the favor."

"You've already saved me, Savannah. You don't have to return anything. I wasn't sure that I'd ever fall in love. I didn't want to. You rescued me from a life spent with one foot out the door."

Gently rubbing her thumb back and forth along Micki's cheekbone, Savannah lost herself in the sincerity pooled in Micki's eyes. She pulled her down again, their bodies erasing any chill in the air, immediately surrounded in heat. Their mouths met in a shower of electricity, a lightning bolt urging them to part their lips, to explore the abyss. Savannah tightened her grip on Micki's hair, pulling her closer, closer because it would never be close enough.

EPILOGUE

One Year Later

Much to Savannah's chagrin, Micki poked at all of the buttons that adorned the steering wheel of her new Infiniti. "Cool," she said as the windshield began to automatically tint against the setting sun.

"Will you stop? I knew I shouldn't have let you drive."

"Oh, come on, we're on our honeymoon, don't you think you should let me have this? This one time?"

Savannah sighed and fell back in her seat. "We're not technically on our honeymoon until we arrive in Niagara Falls," she muttered petulantly.

"I can't even wrap my mind around that fact that it's been a year already," Micki said, looking at the date on Savannah's dash. "One year done in his seven-year sentence. So not enough."

"No, definitely not enough. I wish he hadn't been so cooperative with everything. He should have gotten twenty years at least."

"I know. If only that woman from Iowa had pressed charges. It would have been a whole lot easier to narrow it down to him if he'd had a record for stalking and harassment. I get why she didn't; it can be hard to make a stalking case stick. Maybe he'll be less likely to do it to someone else with a record following him around." Micki shook her head.

"We can only hope. At least the nightmares have finally stopped. Let's not talk about him anymore." Savannah rubbed the sleeve of her sweater. "El was so excited for us to make it official. She told her whole class that Chief Blake was her stepmom now."

Micki smiled at her happily. "I still can't believe it. She's amazing. You're amazing. I'm the luckiest girl in the world," she said, bringing Savannah's hand to her mouth to kiss her fingertips.

Savannah visibly melted. "Yes. Yes, you are. I hope Eliana is having a nice time with my mother. I really want those two to bond. It'll be a lot easier now that she lives in town."

"I think they will. And your mom loves me—of course, how could she not—so I'm sure we'll be seeing her a lot. You two have a lot to catch up on."

"We do. I didn't know how she would feel about walking me down the aisle to marry a woman, but she was amazing. Maybe this really is the fresh start that we've needed." Savannah smiled softly, twisting the diamond on her ring finger.

"A fresh start for all of us, really. Eliana looked so grown up walking down the aisle. And can you believe the way Rebecca cried? You'd have thought she was the mother of the bride, not her best friend."

"I'm still not certain if she was crying because she was losing her best friend or because she was losing her best friend to me. Either way, I'm happy." Savannah flashed her a brilliant smile.

Micki grinned. "It was actually very sweet. Read me your vows again."

"Micki, I've already read them three times."

"It's our honeymoon," Micki said sadly, looking ahead at the road with pitiful eyes.

"Oh, all right." Savannah smirked, pulling the folded piece of stationery out of her purse. She cleared her throat dramatically.

"I wish I could say that from the first moment I saw you, I knew you were the one. I didn't, but I soon learned that you would turn my life upside down. I've never been more right about anything.

"When you walked into my life, you brought love with you. And I know that by having you beside me, I will be a better person tomorrow than I was yesterday.

"I will love you for who you are, not who I want you to be.

"I promise to be patient, understanding, and forgiving—with you but also with myself.

"I will celebrate our triumphs and treat our failures as opportunities.

"I promise to carry you and to be carried by you. You are my best friend and equal.

"I vow to always love you as you deserve to be loved.

"Mackenzie, I believe in us. I am proud to be your wife."

"Every damn time!" Micki used her knuckle to swipe away the moisture beneath her eye. "I still don't fully understand how two people can go from detesting each other to," she gestured between the two of them, "this. You are truly the clichéd, formulaic, platitude-filled love of my life."

"And you're mine."

Sighing happily, Micki sat back, setting the cruise control and removing her foot from the gas. She flipped on the radio, clasping Savannah's hand in her own. Eliana's favorite station, KiddieKat Radio, blared "You Are My Sunshine" throughout the car.

They grasped at the radio buttons, pushing, pulling, lowering, stabbing. The radio went off with a brief stutter of static.

"Huh." Micki laughed uneasily. "Maybe we should just enjoy the silence."

It would take time for the residue of what they'd been through to truly fade away. But for now, life was exactly what it should be.

About the Author

Nicole Stiling lives in New England with her wife, two children, and a menagerie of dogs, cats, and fish. When she's not working at her day job or pounding away at the keyboard, she enjoys video games, comic books, clearing out the DVR, and the occasional amusement park. Nicole is a strict vegetarian who does not like vegetables, and a staunch advocate for anything with four legs.

Books Available From Bold Strokes Books

A Bird of Sorrow by Shea Godfrey. As Darrius and her lover, Princess Jessa, gather their strength for the coming war, a mysterious spell will reveal the truth of an ancient love. (978-1-63555-009-2)

All the Worlds Between Us by Morgan Lee Miller. High school senior Quinn Hughes discovers that a broken friendship is actually a door propped open for an unexpected romance. (978-1-63555-457-1)

An Intimate Deception by CJ Birch. Flynn County Sheriff Elle Ashley has spent her adult life atoning for her wild youth, but when she finds her ex, Jessie, murdered two weeks before the small town's biggest social event, she comes face-to-face with her past and all her well-kept secrets. (978-1-63555-417-5)

Cash and the Sorority Girl by Ashley Bartlett. Cash Braddock doesn't want to deal with morality, drugs, or people. Unfortunately, she's going to have to. (978-1-63555-310-9)

Falling by Kris Bryant. Falling in love isn't part of the plan, but will Shaylie Beck put her heart first and stick around, or tell the damaging truth? (978-1-63555-373-4)

Secrets in a Small Town by Nicole Stiling. Deputy Chief Mackenzie Blake has one mission: find the person harassing Savannah Castillo and her daughter before they cause real harm. (978-1-63555-436-6)

Stormy Seas by Ali Vali. The high-octane follow-up to the best-selling action-romance *Blue Skies*. (978-1-63555-299-7)

The Road to Madison by Elle Spencer. Can two women who fell in love as girls overcome the hurt caused by the father who tore them apart? (978-1-63555-421-2)

Dangerous Curves by Larkin Rose. When love waits at the finish line, dangerous curves are a risk worth taking. (978-1-63555-353-6)

Love to the Rescue by Radclyffe. Can two people who share a past really be strangers? (978-1-62639-973-0)

Love's Portrait by Anna Larner. When museum curator Molly Goode and benefactor Georgina Wright uncover a portrait's secret, public and private truths are exposed, and their deepening love hangs in the balance. (978-1-63555-057-3)

Model Behavior by MJ Williamz. Can one woman's instability shatter a new couple's dreams of happiness? (978-1-63555-379-6)

Pretending in Paradise by M. Ullrich. When travelwisdom.com assigns PR specialist Caroline Beckett and travel blogger Emma Morgan to cover a hot new couples retreat, they're forced to fake a relationship to secure a reservation. (978-1-63555-399-4)

Recipe for Love by Aurora Rey. Hannah Little doesn't have much use for fancy chefs or fancy restaurants, but when New York City chef Drew Davis comes to town, their attraction just might be a recipe for love. (978-1-63555-367-3)

The House by Eden Darry. After a vicious assault, Sadie, Fin, and their family retreat to a house they think is the perfect place to start over, until they realize not all is as it seems. (978-1-63555-395-6)

Uninvited by Jane C. Esther. When Aerin McLeary's body becomes host for an alien intent on invading Earth, she must work with researcher Olivia Ando to uncover the truth and save humankind. (978-1-63555-282-9)

Comrade Cowgirl by Yolanda Wallace. When cattle rancher Laramie Bowman accepts a lucrative job offer far from home, will her heart end up getting lost in translation? (978-1-63555-375-8)

Double Vision by Ellie Hart. When her cell phone rings, Giselle Cutler answers it—and finds herself speaking to a dead woman. (978-1-63555-385-7)

Inheritors of Chaos by Barbara Ann Wright. As factions splinter and reunite, will anyone survive the final showdown between gods and mortals on an alien world? (978-1-63555-294-2)

Spinning Tales by Brey Willows. When the fairy tale begins to unravel and villains are on the loose, will Maggie and Kody be able to spin a new tale? (978-1-63555-314-7)

Love on Lavender Lane by Karis Walsh. Accompanied by the buzz of honeybees and the scent of lavender, Paige and Kassidy must find a way to compromise on their approach to business if they want to save Lavender Lane Farm—and find a way to make room for love along the way. (978-1-63555-286-7)

The Do-Over by Georgia Beers. Bella Hunt has made a good life for herself and put the past behind her. But when the bane of her high school existence shows up for Bella's class on conflict resolution, the last thing they expect is to fall in love. (978-1-63555-393-2)

What Happens When by Samantha Boyette. For Molly Kennan, senior year is already an epic disaster, and falling for mysterious waitress Zia is about to make life a whole lot worse. (978-1-63555-408-3)

Wooing the Farmer by Jenny Frame. When fiercely independent modern socialite Penelope Huntingdon-Stewart and traditional country farmer Sam McQuade meet, trusting their hearts is harder than it looks. (978-1-63555-381-9)

Shut Up and Kiss Me by Julie Cannon. What better way to spend two weeks of hell in paradise than in the company of a hot, sexy woman? (978-1-163555-343-7)

Emily's Art and Soul by Joy Argento. When Emily meets Andi Marino she thinks she's found a new best friend, but Emily doesn't know that Andi is fast falling in love with her. Caught up in exploring her sexuality, will Emily see the only woman she needs is right in front of her? (978-1-163555-355-0)

Spencer's Cove by Missouri Vaun. When Foster Owen and Abigail Spencer meet, they uncover a story of lives adrift, loves lost, and true love found. (978-1-163555-171-6)

Unexpected Lightning by Cass Sellars. Lightning strikes once more when Sydney and Parker fight a dangerous stranger who threatens the peace they both desperately want. (978-1-163555-276-8)

Without Pretense by TJ Thomas. After living for decades hiding from the truth, can Ava learn to trust Bianca with her secrets and her heart? (978-1-163555-173-0)

Escape to Pleasure: Lesbian Travel Erotica, edited by Sandy Lowe and Victoria Villaseñor. Join these award-winning authors as they explore the sensual side of erotic lesbian travel. (978-1-163555-339-0)

Ordinary is Perfect by D. Jackson Leigh. Atlanta marketing superstar Autumn Swan's life derails when she inherits a country home, a child, and a very interesting neighbor. (978-1-163555-280-5)

Royal Court by Jenny Frame. When royal dresser Holly Weaver's passionate personality begins to melt Royal Marine Captain Quincy's icy heart, will Holly be ready for what she exposes beneath? (978-1-163555-290-4)

Strings Attached by Holly Stratimore. Rock star Nikki Razer always gets what she wants, but when she falls for Drew McNally, a music teacher who won't date celebrities, can she convince Drew she's worth the risk? (978-1-163555-347-5)

The Ashford Place by Jean Copeland. When Isabelle Ashford inherits an old house in small-town Connecticut, family secrets, a shocking discovery, and an unexpected romance complicate her plan for a fast profit and a temporary stay. (978-1-163555-316-1)

Treason by Gun Brooke. Zoem Malderyn's existence is a deadly threat to everyone on Gemocon, and Commander Neenja KahSandra must find a way to save the woman she loves from having to make the ultimate sacrifice. (978-1-163555-244-7)

A Wish Upon a Star by Jeannie Levig. Erica Cooper has learned to depend on only herself, but when her new neighbor, Leslie Raymond, befriends Erica's special needs daughter, the walls protecting Erica's heart threaten to crumble. (978-1-163555-274-4)

Answering the Call by Ali Vali. Detective Sept Savoie returns to the streets of New Orleans, as do the dead bodies from ritualistic killings, and she does everything in her power to bring their killers to justice while trying to keep her partner, Keegan Blanchard, safe. (978-1-163555-050-4)